CLAIMING DEMONS

THE SECRETS GODS KEEP: BOOK 3

TESSA COLE

CLARA WILS

Gryphon's Gate Publishing

Gryphon's Gate Publishing
550 King St. N.
PO Box 42088 Conestoga
Waterloo, ON
N2L 6K5

Print ISBN: 978-1-990587-33-7

ANAIS

WAS THIS A DREAM?

It was late, and I'd had the most incredible sex with all my guys, then they'd pampered me and put me to bed. And now, here I was with Harmonia, standing in the middle of one of the main living areas in Grey's apartment, and she'd just said she knew who my mother was.

This had to be a dream.

I reached out and touched Harmonia's Mediterranean-tanned cheek. "You feel real."

"I... what?" She frowned, then rolled her eyes at me. "Ana, this isn't a dream. That theory I was looking into... this is it. It just took me a little longer than expected to find what I was looking for."

Right, she'd said she was looking into something.

But... my mother?

I blinked... and suddenly I needed to sit down.

I staggered toward a couch near the fireplace and

Harmonia helped me to get there. She sat beside me, looking intent, but she waited before saying anything, perhaps looking for some signal from me, some indication that I was ready to hear about my birth mother.

Except I couldn't get any words out and only managed to nod, indicating that I was as good as I was going to get for this information.

"There are many goddesses out there, but not many with the slew of aspects that you possess," she said, keeping her gaze locked with mine. "As soon as you manifested war, that drastically reduced the options. There aren't many goddesses of sex and war, and I assumed both of those were aspects from your mother, but then... that's where the research came in."

My thoughts whirled, despite Harmonia's gaze keeping me steady.

She knew who my mother was.

She *knew* who my mother was.

"It was your aspect of healing which was confusing," she continued as if she couldn't feel the tangle of emotions roaring through me like I knew she could. "It didn't match up with the others. So, once I pulled that out of the mix and presumed that healing had come from your father... that led me to my theory. Which proved to be correct."

I waited, holding my breath as Harmonia let that sink in.

But, of course, it couldn't, because she. Knew. Who. My. Mother. Was.

"I'm almost certain your mother was Inanna," she finished, since I'd just continued to stare at her blankly.

Inanna.

My mother was Inanna.

Who the hell was Inanna? I'd never heard of her. Of course, I hadn't heard of a lot of gods and goddesses, but still... the revelation I'd hoped for hadn't arrived. I was still confused.

"Who is she?" I asked.

Then I caught onto what she'd said a moment ago: your mother *was* Inanna. As in past tense. As in... dead?

I had no idea how I felt about that, either.

"Who *was* she?" I forced out.

"One of the first and most powerful goddesses from the ancient Sumerian pantheon. Her aspects were love, beauty, sex, fertility, war, and law."

Then realization hit me. "Law!" I blurted out. Of course! "*That*'s what Reia has!"

The aspect that I hadn't been able to name, that had felt related to war, was law. Fighting for justice was a battle, much like war.

"Most likely," Harmonia replied with a gentle nod.

Oh, my gods! I knew my mother's name. She was a goddess I'd never heard of, but that didn't mean I couldn't do research, learn more about her, discover—

Wait. Everything I'd find in the history books or talking to other daemons was great, but the whole point of figuring out who my parents were was to discover more about me.

"What does this mean?" I asked.

"There's more to Inanna's tale," Harmonia said softly. "And it's why I'm certain Inanna is your mother." She paused, her look telling me to brace myself. "Your mother — Inanna — died almost forty years ago. The rumor is, she died in childbirth."

Almost forty years?

I was thirty-eight.

"Oh..." I blinked. "She died... having me?" That didn't make any sense. "But... she was a goddess of fertility. How's that possible?"

"That's the thing, no one knows for certain," Harmonia said. "We know Inanna died, but there is no record of her death. The rumor is she died in childbirth, but as you say, that doesn't make much sense. The trouble is, there isn't much more to go on. There's no record of the father, nor the identity of the child. It's all a little vague and mysterious. Someone went to a lot of trouble to conceal the details of this."

And that struck a chord with me. "My adoption records... They mysteriously went missing. Only mine."

"Someone didn't want you, or anyone else, to figure this out."

"I'm guessing that was my father?" I said, my tone rising, making it more of a question than a statement. "But why?"

"I don't know. And there's more. Usually, the child of a god or goddess has only some of their parents' powers, or sometimes they have new powers. It's extremely rare for a child to have identical powers to their parents," Harmonia continued, her gaze drifting to the window and the sparkling Manhattan skyline beyond. "Yet, there are tales that goddesses who die giving birth sometimes pass all their powers on to their child. I think that's what happened with you."

"Oh." I wasn't sure why that was significant. It explained my rather extensive list of aspects, but still... "Is that... everything?"

Harmonia nodded. "That's everything I could find so far. Together, we can look into this, find out more. Though, it sounds like someone went through a lot of trouble to keep all of this hidden from you."

"Or..." I said as another possibility occurred to me. "Someone did this to keep *me* hidden from the world."

Harmonia's eyes went wide, surprise then fear flickered across her expression before she returned to her usual serene self.

"That's a possibility," she said as she pulled my hands from my lap, holding them firmly clasped between hers. "I'm sorry to drop this all on you in the middle of the night. Would you like me to soothe you so you can get back to sleep, or do you want to sit with this for a while?"

What did I want?

I wanted to know more — now now now.

But it had only been two days since I'd battled zompires and fought Nari and Melinoe. And I was still groggy from last night's activities. If I stayed up, I'd only spend the day being foggy-headed and probably not get much done.

There wasn't anything more we would find out tonight, and Harmonia had already been digging into this for a full day. It could wait, as much as I didn't want it to.

"Put me to sleep," I said, shaking my head. "I'm certain I won't be able to sleep without your help."

She rose and helped me lie on the couch, covering me with a blanket and kneeling next to me.

"We'll find out more," she whispered reassuringly as she stroked my hair and I felt her power working on me, my cares and worries draining away. "We'll solve this mystery and get you all the answers you desire... later. Sleep for now, dear friend."

I woke when Reia — and a bounding Kerberos — strode through the common space of the penthouse on their way out for their morning run.

I didn't think they knew I was out there, and they didn't say anything, so I stayed bundled in my blanket and watched the sun crest the horizon in the east.

The view was amazing from the high vantage point of Grey's penthouse, and I felt rested enough to get up and start making coffee and breakfast.

As I did, I tried to make sense of what Harmonia had told me, my thoughts spinning from being a goddess, to my mother's death, to my still-mysterious father, and how someone was clearly trying to cover it all up.

Does this change anything? I asked myself

No... it didn't.

I knew the name of my birth mother and that she'd given me all her powers. I'd hoped to track down my birth parents, find out more from them, but I wouldn't be able to do that now. So, I was left with just a name, which was precious little more than I'd known before.

And since I knew so little still, I didn't want to mention anything to the guys, or Reia and Eva. I'd find out what I could, then let everyone know. Still, I got out my little notebook and jotted down this new information.

Eva, Trent, and Trent's sister Lisa — carrying her little one — were up next. Trent scarfed down some toast then, on his way out, Eva captured him in the front hall and they smooched like young lovers. After he'd left, Lisa began nursing her baby and an awkward silence settled over the group of us. That suited me just fine. I had a lot to think about.

Donny was up next, and he grabbed an apple to go, his new job consulting for Grey's financial sector keeping him busy. A little while after that, Reia returned, huffing, sweating, and smiling, and Kerberos bounded to me, tongue lolling out, ready to bowl me over.

"Down!" Reia commanded, and the huge dog stopped instantly.

Pride swelled in my chest. That was my little girl commanding a hellhound. I should have been surprised, but with Reia, very little surprised me these days.

"Good doggy," I said, patting Kerberos' huge head.

Kerberos spun and bounded back to Reia and together they headed to her room.

By the time she'd showered and returned for breakfast, the guys were up.

We all ate in a sort of reverent silence, and I didn't know why the rest of them were so quiet, but I appreciated it.

Reia left for school. Eva headed out to look into military academies. Fen and Ramsey both kissed me as if this were both the first and last times we might ever touch lips, and then they headed to their jobs — Ramsey taking Lisa with him to start her divorce proceedings.

That left Grey.

"What do you need?" he asked me, his expression soft as if he could tell there was something on my mind.

"Some time, peace and quiet?"

He nodded. "Let me know if you need me for anything."

"A hug," I said, going to him and wrapping my arms around him. "I'll always need a hug."

He held me silently, strong arms enfolding me in his warmth. Freshly showered, he smelled like sandalwood and cedar with a hint of eucalyptus. I drank in his scent and stayed there in his arms for a long time.

He didn't complain or ask why or when I'd be done, he just held me as long as I needed it. And with everything that had happened, I needed a while.

When I finally drew back, he whispered, "Last night was... incredible, and you are... exceptional. I love you, Anais Baker."

Then he kissed me lightly and smiled. The swirling

void in his dark-sable eyes almost seemed to vanish, but not quite, which reminded me that I'd promised to help him control it so he could turn it off when he didn't want it.

"I love you too, Grey," I said, the words coming remarkably easy.

I didn't know if it was because I'd tapped into my aspect of love, or whether the news from last night had perhaps changed me a little, but I'd accepted that I could love... and be loved.

And that was a far greater boon than knowing who my mother might have been.

I pulled him close for another quick hug, then let him go, feeling livelier and lighthearted.

I made a trip to my house later that morning. I wanted to pick up a few more things, and Donny had said the renovation contractor would be there, so I could make sure they were doing what we wanted with the place.

When I arrived, dozens of men were getting set up. And, with me in a body-hugging, cream, long-sleeved top, a knee-length, grey-and-white tartan skirt, and black, knee-high stockings, I was turning all their heads.

I found the foreman in Reia's room measuring for where my new bathroom would be. Part of the remodel was giving me — and my guys, when they were here — more room. My bedroom and closets would be expanded and I'd have a large bathroom where Reia's bedroom was now. Reia would move up into a mini-suite on the top floor.

There would also still be a secondary, small bedroom up there for guests, as well as the suite in the basement, where Grey had been staying.

I talked to the foreman and we reviewed the designs he'd drawn up. I changed a few things, mostly minor. Then I collected the clothes I'd come to get — which were more than I'd thought — and ended up packing three large suitcases.

Luckily there was no shortage of men willing to help me carry them downstairs.

As I was about to leave, someone knocked on the front door, and when I opened it, I gaped, blinking in surprise.

"Hey, Mom," Caia — my eldest daughter — said casually. "I'm home!"

ANAIS

"CAIA!" I SAID... WHICH WAS PRETTY INANE.

I blinked as I tried to work through what this meant. It was November, and she should be in school... at Harvard.

Oh... no!

"You weren't expelled, were you?" Caia had always been studious and driven. I couldn't imagine she'd done anything worthy of expulsion, but—

"What? No!" She laughed. "This was my last term and I'm pretty much done except for a few papers I can send in by email. I'll have to go back for exams, but I thought I'd come home for a bit." She looked around at the construction workers filling the house. Then she spied the three heavy suitcases some of those men were holding for me. "Is... everything okay here?"

"Ah... no, we're remodeling. But that's okay, we're staying downtown in a penthouse now."

Caia raised her brows. "Swanky. I always knew Great-uncle Donny was loaded, but... wow."

"Actually..." I gave her my winningest grin because I knew how this was going to sound. "It's my boyfriend's place."

Caia's face fell. "Oh."

"It's not like that, not anymore," I said. "I've found a really good one."

Three of them actually, but that could wait for now.

"Why don't you come and meet him? That's his car there, waiting for me." I pointed at the Bentley Mulsanne Grand Limousine waiting at the side of the street. I could see her hesitation. "Come with me and let me explain. There's a lot to explain, but Uncle Donny, Reia, and even Eva are all staying there right now. So it can't be that bad, right?"

"Eva's back?"

I nodded.

"Oh."

Yeah, that wasn't a selling point for Caia. She and Eva had never seen eye to eye.

"She's mellowed a lot." *Since she found out she was a daemon of war.*

That was another discussion Caia and I needed to have.

This was going to be a long morning.

Caia shrugged. "Sure, let's go."

Grey's chauffeur loaded Caia's things and my three heavy suitcases into the massive trunk, and Caia and I settled into the back of the car. I took one of the back-facing seats so we could have this conversation eye-to eye. The privacy window — between the front and back of the car — was already up, so I felt comfortable speaking openly with my daughter.

Once the driver had pulled out and we were on our way, I jumped into the first of two difficult discussions, starting with the more mundane one.

"So... I'm not just seeing one guy right now. I'm seeing three," I said. "It's a polyamorous thing. They're all okay with it and they all love me and it's... wonderful!"

Caia blinked her large green eyes at me. She combed a hand through her straight, silver hair — like mine, but hers was cut short in a chin-length bob — and blew out a breath.

"Oh?" she finally replied.

"Yup."

"And we're going to stay with one of these guys, or do all three of them live there?"

"The penthouse is owned by just one, Grey. But the others visit... a lot," I told her. "The other two have nice places, too. Did I mention they're all stupidly rich?"

"Nope," she said, her tone flat.

"Grey owns like a billion businesses, Ramsey is a lawyer, and Fen has a high-end restaurant and a construction business," I added, my tone getting bubblier and bubblier, but my sales pitch was falling on deaf ears.

"Sounds... eclectic." Her lips were tight. I could tell she wasn't impressed. But then, I'd never brought home a single winner when she'd been growing up, so why would she suspect anything had changed?

"Look, I know I dated a lot of losers," I said, sighing heavily. "And I know, in the past, I told you to 'just give them a try' even when they were losers. But I've changed. A lot — we'll get to that discussion in a moment — and these guys are different too. They... worship me, which I don't really understand, but they do. Just meet them and judge for yourself, okay? If you don't want to stay with us, we'll find a hotel for you."

She grimaced and nodded, still not convinced. "Sure, fine, whatever."

What a resounding endorsement.

Now for the second and even harder discussion.

"So... like I said a moment ago, I've changed a lot recently." I tried to keep smiling, not letting my trepidation affect my voice. "There really isn't an easy way to say this, so... here goes. It turns out I'm a goddess."

Caia raised a skeptical brow, but I pushed on before she could comment.

"All the gods in all the pantheons you've ever heard of are real and so are lesser celestial beings known as daemons. I thought I was a daemon at first, but they only have two aspects, and I have—" I counted quickly. "—at least six, which makes me a goddess. The guys I'm dating are all daemons. Well, they're daemon princes actually. They have two aspects and they're really old and powerful, and what this all means is that all my daughters have aspects too. You have powers, like me.

Eva has sex and war. Reia has law, and you... probably have some too." I paused at that point, trying to gauge Caia's response.

Much to my surprise, her skepticism had faded a little.

"Huh..." she said softly, brow furrowed in thought. "That... would explain a lot."

"It would?" She seemed to be accepting this far too easily.

"Do you have powers around love and medicine or healing?" she asked.

"Ah... yeah... why?" Though as soon as I asked, I knew why.

"All the guys at school, and some of the girls for that matter, are all falling-over-themselves in love with me. Also, I seem to be able to heal myself and others. I thought I was just crazy or a mutant or something, but now ..." She blinked. "I still don't really believe any of it, and half of what you just said doesn't make any sense... but, hey. Maybe I'm *not* crazy. This explains why those things have been happening."

"Yeah," I said. "Sorry, my fault."

"And Eva is sex and war? That explains soooo much. No wonder we never got along." Caia cocked her head. "Does that mean you're a goddess of war?"

"Yup. I'm pretty badass."

I summoned my mystical glowing sword to show Caia. She flinched, her eyes flashing wide.

"Fuck, Mom!"

I made it go away. "So... yeah. I know, a lot to take in. Take your time. I'm just glad you're home, Caia."

She smiled, though it seemed a bit forced. "Yeah, time... I think I'll need that... and probably many more long talks." Then she laughed. "But yeah, I'm glad to be home too, even if it's not *at* home."

Something told me she wouldn't be complaining too much when she saw Grey's place.

ANAIS

I GOT CAIA SETTLED IN A LUXURIOUS GUEST ROOM AND deposited my suitcases in Grey's room, which was now essentially my room too.

By the time I was done putting my stuff away in Grey's massive, walk-in closet, I found Caia in the main living area chatting with Grey. He hadn't been here when we'd arrived and must have returned while I was busy in the closet.

He wore a casual-looking suit, dark grey, with his usual black shirt, the collar open. His thick black hair was perfectly combed back, and he was sexy as ever. Those sable eyes caught mine as I drew near and he smiled.

"Your daughter is extremely astute," he said. "We've been talking business strategies and she has some interesting ideas. I shouldn't be surprised since she's a Harvard grad."

"I haven't graduated yet," Caia said a bit flushed from being put on the spot.

Grey cocked his head at her modesty. "You're in your last semester, having fast-tracked through a double major in business and medicine, and your GPA is what?"

"Four-point-oh," she said a bit sheepishly.

"I thought so." Grey smiled. "Back when I was more actively running my businesses, I would have snapped you up in an instant. I have a bio-medical research branch that could use an innovative young mind like yours."

Caia looked at me. "Is he for real?"

"Yup." I settled onto the couch next to Grey and kissed his cheek. "He's very real and very perfect, and he loves me like the goddess I am." I snuggled into him a little, feeling the warmth of his tall frame next to mine. I didn't care that my daughter was in the room. Let her see how much we loved each other.

I said to Grey, "Caia tells me everyone at school is head-over-heels in love with her and she can heal, so she probably has my aspects of love and healing."

"That makes you a daemon princess," Grey said to Caia, nodding. "Technically on par with me."

"What are your... ah... aspects?" Caia asked. She still seemed hesitant with the terminology, but was catching on quickly.

"Hunting and acquisition. My title is The Lord of Conquest."

"Oh... ah... wow..." Caia seemed a bit lost for words, but she recovered quickly. "Do you hunt animals?"

"I do, but never to kill. I hunt with my bare hands and my intellect to trap and release." His grin softened. "I love animals almost as much as I love your mother. One of the businesses I'll never give up is my network of animal shelters."

"You should see him around those poor animals," I cooed. "He becomes the biggest softy you've ever seen."

Caia blinked, probably having a hard time imagining big, hunky Grey turning into a puddle of saccharine goo at the sight of kittens. But I'd seen it with my own eyes.

She frowned, her head tilting to the side. "I can sense your love for each other. I'm... happy." Then she laughed, shaking her head. "This is a lot to get used to."

"Take your time," Grey said softly, understanding. "Your mother was a hot mess when she first found out."

I slapped him playfully. "You're not supposed to say that! My daughters idolize me."

Caia let out a very unprofessional snort, which made us all laugh.

I sighed as the moment faded. "I know I wasn't a great mother, Caia. I'm sorry."

Caia gave me a forgiving look. "You may have dated a lot of losers — and I mean *a lot*, like every loser on the Eastern Seaboard — and you may have been a bit distant at times, but when it really counted, when I really needed you, you were there for me," she said.

It was my turn to flush a little, warmed by her praise.

"Your advice was horrible." She shook her head and rolled her eyes. "But you tried."

"Gee, thanks," I said with a laugh, because my advice probably *had* been horrible.

She looked away for a moment, lost in memories. "I can remember you holding me, comforting me, after I'd gotten my first A-minus in fourth grade." Then she gave a bit of a head-shaking laugh. "And in high school, you threatened to have one of your goon boyfriends go beat up James Wilson after he broke my heart."

"I'll never understand that," I told her, still upset even though it had happened years ago. "You're perfect! So smart and beautiful."

"I was also flat as a board and he left me for Brina Butler, with her perky double-Ds," she said with a wry grin.

Caia had my height and my silver hair, but that was where our physical resemblance stopped. She was slender and willowy with long elegant arms and legs, but not much in the way of curves. She had the physique of a model and had actually done some modeling to help pay for school.

I couldn't believe that silly boy had dumped her.

"Boys are idiots. Aren't they Grey?" I challenged him.

"Absolutely. Most men are idiots too," he said easily.

That made Caia smile.

We continued to chat over lunch and through the afternoon, though Caia and Grey often took long tangents into business and medicine and things I didn't understand.

Then Reia got home from school and was overjoyed to see Caia. She offered to show Caia some nearby sights as she walked Kerberos.

I saw them off, but when I turned back to Grey — standing in the front hall behind me — he had the oddest smile on his lips, like he was thinking through some drawn-out, brilliant idea.

"What?" I asked him.

"What would you say if I offered my empire to Caia?"

"Ahhhhhhhhhh." It was like my mind had shut down. I knew words existed and I should have used some, but I couldn't stop gaping at him.

"I've talked with her enough to know she's brilliant," he said with a grin. "I think she'd do well as CEO of Zagreus Holdings International, or at least my bio-medical division. Maybe I'll start her off there, with the intent to groom her into the CEO?"

"You... really think she could do it?"

His sable-void eyes met mine. "Don't you?"

Ouch.

He'd known my daughter all of one afternoon and already seemed to know her better than I did.

"I know she can do anything," I told him. "I just didn't think she'd do it... this soon."

Grey kissed me softly, a quick brush of his lips that sent tingling sparks rushing through my veins.

"She's ready," he breathed, then pulled me close. His

next kiss was far less tentative, and the sparks in my blood turned to flames, sweeping through me. "Are you ready to let her go?" he whispered when he drew back.

My mind was addled by that passionate kiss, and I blinked for a moment before I fully registered his question.

Was I ready to let her go?

The answer surprised me.

No... I wasn't.

I'd been a horrible mother, and I wanted a chance to change that, to spend quality time with my girls now that I knew a bit more about myself.

Except it might be too late.

Caia was twenty-one, a grown woman, and didn't really need me anymore. Eva was finding her own way in the world, and Reia... she'd never needed me. The sad truth was: I needed my girls far more than they needed me.

"I'm not ready to let go of any of them. I... I want to spend more time with them."

I vowed to do just that, and get to know them as they were now, as women coming into their own.

Grey smiled, the void of his eyes swirling with greater intensity. "Then I guess I'll have to get my time with you when I can."

His hand curved over my butt then urged me to raise my knee. I slid my leg up and his fingers slid down under my skirt to trace lines of electric pleasure over my folds.

I'd pretty much given up on panties and it was a good

thing too, because Grey's expert fingers quickly had my pussy drooling and hungry for more. He pinned me against the wall as his fingers attacked my clit, and his lips devoured mine. His hard body pressed close in all the right ways.

A soft-shuddering, soothing orgasm sang through my body and ramped up my desire from *burning* to *savage*. I mewled and moaned into his mouth. I hadn't even accessed my sex aspect, but we were both on fire.

He pulled back long enough to free his rigid cock and slip on a condom. Apparently, he kept some on him at all times… just in case.

My voice was already hoarse as I whispered, "You don't need that now, I can control—"

"I don't want to make a mess," he said heatedly.

Oh… right.

That brought to mind his epic surge inside me last night and I nearly came just from remembering it. The instant he had that condom on, I pulled myself up, arms around his neck, legs around his waist, and he plunged into me.

Caia and Reia would probably be gone for a little while, but we had no clue when Eva would be home, so, I ground down on him hard, rubbing my clit against him while tapping into my sex to make my pussy clench and pulse, squeezing his shaft relentlessly.

He must have felt the urgency too, as his thrusts quickly escalated, pounding into my pussy, slamming my clit, and driving me mad.

His lips dominated mine, and when I was swept into the torrent of my next powerful orgasm, I cried out into his soul, letting him know how amazing I felt and how much I wanted him to join me.

He grunted with a final crushing thrust and his cock pulsed over and over with his release.

Yes! Oh gods, yes! I doused us both in heated sex and connected us with love which made our combined bliss explode through us, reverberating like church bells.

We clung to each other for a long moment, trembling, foreheads together, breathing into the heated space between our faces, nibbling on each other's lips.

"Eva could be home anytime," I whispered, though I wasn't making any moves to disengage from him.

"She's a daemon of sex, she'll understand."

I chuckled. He was right. *She'd* think nothing of this. *I* was the one who didn't want her to see me this way.

"Still," I breathed, and reluctantly began climbing off him. "Perhaps a change of location instead of the front hall?"

I took his hand and led him to the bedroom... and then the shower.

Grey stripped me slowly, kissing every part of me, getting me all stoked and desperate before he quickly slid out of his suit and we crushed ourselves together under the steamy waters.

He pleasured me relentlessly with hands and lips, prompting a series of ever-escalating orgasms. Then, he turned me around and slid his rigid cock into my ass.

With one hand on my pussy — two fingers inside and his palm pressing to my clit — and his other hand kneading a ragingly sensitive breast, he made me come over and over before finally finding his own release and shattering my world with a powerful mutual orgasm.

By the time we left the bedroom, Eva had returned. She took one look at us and grinned.

"You two didn't get enough last night?" she asked knowingly.

With her sex aspect, we wouldn't have been able to hide it from her if we tried. As it was, the entire penthouse was probably billowing with our lust.

Eva laughed. "I won't tell anyone. Just don't complain when I'm having my own screaming orgasms with Trent later, deal?" She winked at us.

I changed the topic. "How was your search for schools?"

She beamed. "Great. I've applied for the New York Military Academy, with the hopes of going from there to West Point."

"Oh... wow," I said. "All that in one day?"

"Yup," she said, certain. "I'm going to get changed and go see Trent to tell him the plan. We may be out late... celebrating." She laughed and headed to her room.

"Good for her," Grey said behind me, coming up to wrap strong arms around me and kissing my still-damp hair.

"I'm happy she's found a direction," I said.

But then, remembering my desire to get to know my

kids before they left... *and* before I had three frick'n *more* kids... I hoped Eva wouldn't be leaving right away. I vowed again to make the most of the time I had.

Eva left about the same time Caia and Reia returned. We had a nice dinner together, then Ramsey and Fen showed up. Ramsey had set Lisa up in a high-end hotel with a security detail so she'd be safe from her ex.

Caia and Reia went down into the den to relax as my guys and I claimed the living room. But I quickly sensed that sex wasn't on their minds.

The three of them shared a knowing look.

"What...?" I asked.

Fen was stoic and serious when he said, "We need to talk."

ANAIS

Had they found out about my mother? I didn't think Harmonia would tell them without my permission, but... what else could this be?

"Every five years," Fen said, "on the second weekend in November, Empyreans hold a conclave, a gathering, where they discuss matters and work out disagreements in a neutral forum. This year it's in New York."

I blinked. Of all the things they could have said, I'd never have guessed that.

"And...?" I prompted with a shrug. I didn't know what this had to do with me. Yes, I was a goddess, but did I *have* to go to this thing or could I just skip it?

The three of them looked at each other.

"*And...* it's a big deal," Grey said slowly. "Also, if you want to meet a lot of gods and daemons, in hopes of figuring out who your parents are, there won't be a better time or place."

"Ah." So Harmonia hadn't told them of her revelation.

They thought I was still looking... and I was... but only for my father now. My father... who might have all the answers and know why I'd been hidden away from the world.

Okay, now I was interested in this conclave thing.

"How does one get invited?" I asked.

"As long as you're an Empyrean, you're in," Ramsey replied. "We just wanted to let you know so you could prepare."

"Prepare?"

"Your control of your powers has come a long way, but you still... leak occasionally," Fen said with a shrug. "We want to help you make sure you come across as in control and powerful. That means you have two weeks to lock down your powers and become the regal goddess all three of us know you are."

I smiled. *Hell yeah, I am!*

I turned to Grey. "We can also use that time to get your void under control if you like."

He nodded. "Yes, thank you."

"For that matter, both your chaos—" I said to Ramsey, then turned to Fen, "—and your beast seem to have been coming out a lot. Do you need more control?"

"Probably," Fen admitted.

Ramsey just grunted.

We all considered that for a long moment before Ramsey said, "As daemon princes of the host city, a lot of the preparations for this event are falling on us. We're going to be very busy over the next little while and may not be around much. That's the main reason we're telling you all this." He grinned. "Because... we're all free tonight."

I instantly warmed, a low simmer of heat thrumming through me at the thought of another night with my three guys.

"Oh?" I breathed.

"Though, I do want some alone time with you," Ramsey admitted.

"I don't care," Fen said with a shrug. "I'm good with alone or with others."

Grey gave me a smile that spoke volumes: *I've already pleasured you plenty today, but I wouldn't mind more.*

I shivered with anticipation. I absolutely *loved* when all three were with me at the same time.

Hopping to my feet, I said, "One sec, boys." Going to my wallet, I grabbed all the cash I had, then raced down-stairs to find Reia and Caia.

"Hey girls, ah... here's some cash, go out and have fun." It was a Friday, so I didn't mind telling my school-aged kid to go out.

"Need some alone time with your three hunks?" Reia asked in mock innocence, blinking her long eyelashes.

"Yes." Why try to hide it? "They're going to be busy over the next few weeks, this may be the last time I have with them for a while."

Caia's eyes widened. "Things *have* changed. Before it

was all scumbags and secrecy, now it's hunks and honesty. Good for you, Mom."

I didn't know why compliments from my daughters made me feel so good, but they did.

"I have no clue where to go on a Friday night," Reia said. "I'll text Eva and find out." To Caia, she asked, "You want to go upscale or slum it?"

"Upscale. I should get changed."

"You can use Grey's car and chauffeur if you want," I added.

"Then definitely upscale." Reia nodded, fingers flying over her phone.

A half-hour later — which would have been record time if it were me, but both these girls were naturally beautiful and didn't need much to make them dazzle — they were on their way out.

Caia was stunning in an aqua-blue, backless body-con dress. Reia wore a black silk blouse and black dress pants.

Even going clubbing, Reia wouldn't wear a dress.

I told them to have fun and be safe. The old "don't do anything I wouldn't do" advice had never worked for me. And once they'd left, I returned to my guys.

"I get you first," Ramsey said, his low, gravelly voice filled with anticipation as he rose from the couch.

"Then?" I prompted. I was curious how they'd planned things, loving how they worked so well together.

"Then I get some time alone, while Ramsey recovers," Fen said. "Then all three of us."

Hell yes, I could get behind this plan!

I was all set to hurry into the bedroom with Ramsey, but he didn't let me get that far. He captured me in a bear hug, crushing me against him as his lips claimed mine in a hungry, ferocious kiss. Apparently, we were going to start right here.

He pushed me up against a wall in the living room — which got me thinking of my time with Grey that afternoon. But this was different, hard and rough, knocking the air out of me.

One of his large hands came to my chest and ravaged a breast through my shirt. He was brutish and driven, and gods, I loved it! This *was* Ramsey and all his furious need.

His mouth left mine, his stubble scratching my cheek as he moved to bite an earlobe.

"I'm going to make you come and make them watch," he growled.

Apparently, alpha Ramsey was going to show his dominance. I'd play along, especially since I was going to get an orgasm out of the deal.

He spun us around so his back was against the wall, and his hands slid down to flip up my skirt and clamp onto my ass, pressing me close. I felt the massive bulge of his erection crushed between us and rocked my hips a little to tease him.

He grunted and smashed his mouth to mine once again, sucking and licking with a passion that built a frenzy within me. His hands gripped and fondled my ass, right in front of Grey and Fen. It wasn't like they were strangers or hadn't seen me naked before, but there was still a thrill to have Ramsey claiming me with them watching.

Then, surprisingly, Ramsey spun me around. Now my back was to his chest and I was facing Grey and Fen.

Oh! Now, this was interesting indeed!

"Lift your left leg," Ramsey whispered from behind me.

I did, and he grabbed it with his left arm pulling it up till my knee was against my chest, once again showing my dripping folds to my other two lovers.

Fen's eyes darkened with desire and the muscles in Grey's jaw twitched.

Ramsey leaned heavily over my shoulder and turned my face to his, seizing my lips in a way only Ramsey could, breathless and burning with desire. Then he reached down with his right hand and began an assault on my clit.

Fire erupted in my body, blazing through my blood, his passion bearing down on me like a tidal wave, crashing over me and carrying me away in its flood. My insides turned to lava, heat searing through me, and my core clenched with urgency, desperate to be filled.

His strength and ferocious need dominated me. I was trapped in his grasp, his massive body so much stronger and bigger than mine, and all I could do was hold on for the ride.

Ramsey rubbed my clit furiously, twisting my need

tight. And when he plunged two thick fingers inside me, I came... hard.

My eyes rolled back and I screamed my release, my hips bucking against his hand.

Ramsey grunted with masculine satisfaction and relentlessly finger-fucked me all through my gushing orgasm.

And when I was done, legs weak, he gave another grunt, threw me over his shoulder, and carried me away like some caveman claiming his bride.

"Bring it on, big boy," I whispered to Ramsey with a giggle.

He gave a heavy, playful grunt, which I felt deep in my gut, sending shivering aftershocks up my spine.

Oh, yeah. This was going to be good!

RAMSEY

N<small>O ONE COULD DO VISCERAL, PRIMAL, CAVEMAN SEX LIKE</small> I could.

"Just don't rip off this outfit, I really like it," Ana said as we entered the bedroom.

"So do I," I growled as I pulled her off my shoulder, holding her aloft easily in my hands.

Her eyes glazed over for a moment with a flush of desire, and I smirked with satisfaction. She was still riding the wave of the orgasm I'd given her.

"Strip, cavewoman," I demanded as I threw her on the bed, before quickly pulling off my clothes.

I didn't have a spare suit with me, so as much as I wanted to rip off my clothes in true caveman style, this would have to do.

Ana seemed to have some super-speed when it came to clothes removal and was waiting, naked on the bed, by the time I'd shed all my things. She lay there, like some cover model on an X-rated pulp fiction novel with her silver hair splayed around her head, silver-blue eyes pleading, and lips pouting, begging to be ravished.

She was half on her side, her chest thrust out, one hand outstretched toward me, and the other was lazily draped over her stomach, her baby finger a breath away from her curls. Her legs were open, one laying bent on the bed, the other propped up, revealing her gleaming juices all over her thighs from my aggressive fingering earlier, and that made my already rock-hard cock swell and twitch.

But I hesitated before going to her.

As much as I'd wanted to show Grey and Fen my dominance, making her mine, when I was alone with Ana, all I really wanted was for *her* to command *me*.

Ever since she'd used that bondage gear on me in her basement, it was all I could think about.

I absentmindedly fingered my nipple-piercing as I watched Ana... and that reminded me...

"I got you a present," I said, sliding my hand down to my cock-ring. I'd replaced the barbell with a ring, studded with small balls. It would stimulate her clit during face-to-face sex and I couldn't wait to try it out.

Ana's eyes widened.

I loved that look.

I climbed onto the bed and knelt next to her.

Her outstretched arm reached up, her finger sliding under the bottom of my cock, teasing me, making my chaos swirl in anticipation. I let her stroke me for a moment, savoring the feel of her small hand on me.

"I want you to get me right to the edge," I said, voice gruff. "Like last time, when I was about to come, but you stopped me. I want to feel that exquisite pain of not being able to come as I give you rough caveman sex."

"I like the sound of that," she said, her lips curling in a wicked grin as she leaned forward and took the tip of my cock in her mouth.

Her silver hair tumbled across her face and I grabbed a handful of it, so I could watch my cock sink deeper and deeper into her until her nose was pressed against my new piercing. Her cheeks were flushed and she stared up at me, her silver-blue eyes burning with desire.

Then she slowly pulled back, revealing my cock, inch by inch, moaning like I tasted like heaven.

Gods, she was so fucking sexy.

She plunged down my length, swallowing while I was impossibly deep in her throat, her muscles squeezing tight around me.

I groaned my pleasure as she licked and sucked and her breathing picked up, ragged gasps through her nose that rushed hot air against my skin.

Fuck, she felt so good. I grabbed one of her tits and kneaded it roughly, loving the pliant warmth of that perky flesh and the feel of her hard nipple digging into my palm. I was already hard from making her come in front of Fen and Grey, and with her amazing oral work, it wasn't long before I was ready to blow.

"Yes! Now!" I grunted.

I shot a stream of cum into her mouth before I felt that constriction around my base. My cock twitched again and again, trying to continue its release, but it couldn't. I gave a keening groan at the painful pleasure of this perfectly poised peak.

Fuck!

My entire body and soul screamed with restrained need as Ana popped off me and looked up with a wicked grin.

"Take me, my caveman. Slam your massive club into my dripping cave."

She rolled over, bringing her knees under her, raising her ass, her face pressed sideways to the mattress.

"Come on, big boy. Take me."

She wiggled her ass and my caveman fully took over. As much as I wanted to find out what my cock-ring did, I had to take her from behind, primal and hard, now now now.

My cock ached, swollen beyond its usual monstrous limits, but I needed to be sure she was ready for me. I shoved two fingers inside her, found her g-spot, and slammed my fingers against it until she was screaming into the sheets and gushing with hot juices. Then I withdrew my fingers, grabbed her hips, and with a single hard thrust buried my cock to the hilt inside her.

Her screams rose an octave, and she levered herself up onto her arms, body taut and rigid as I took her with ferocious thrusts. The pressure-pain squeezing my cock pounded with my pulse, hard and heavy, and my chaos sung, surging through my veins.

I slid my hands down her flanks, bending over until I had her heavy tits in my palms. Then I lifted her, back to my chest, feeling the stimulating shift as her pussy adjusted around me.

"You're my woman," I snarled in her ear, squeezing her tits and thrusting all the harder.

I could see her face, contorted in wide-eyed, mouth-gaping bliss. Her body shook heavily in my arms, her cum was flowing like a river around my cock, and my caveman roared with victory.

Gods, she was perfect. She might be my woman in this moment, but I'd be her man *forever*. And I was the luckiest man in the world — well, one of three — because of that.

"You have control," I whispered, reminding her. "When you want me to come, just release me."

Her panting, heaving breaths became a sort of rough laugh.

"Not... yet... caveman," she gasped before switching to her soul-voice. *My needs run deep and you're doing a great job of satisfying them, but this cavewoman needs... more.*

With that, she kicked back with her hips, adding to my heavy thrusts. She was nearly as wild as I was.

Gasping and crying, she tore one of my hands off her chest and slid it down to her clit, pressing my fingers hard against her bucking loins.

Now... keep that up and carry me into the bathroom, she demanded.

I rose carefully, lifting her easily while keeping pressure on her clit and chest, her legs fell away, useless, once I was on the floor. She was tall — not as tall as I was — but it wasn't easy to walk and fuck. Somehow, I managed to keep a steady rhythm as I took her into the bathroom.

Shower stall, fuck me against the wall, caveman.

I obeyed, slipping my hands to her hips as I pressed her front to the tiles and continued my barrage on her pussy.

After that, her inner voice was all screams and shouts of bliss... as was her outer voice.

Then, she seemed to reach some next level of orgasm and went silent and almost still, her body quivering with a powerful release.

I heard a faint gasping-giggle inside me, and without warning, she released the hold on my cock. The full release of my orgasm slammed into me so hard I was stunned. My roar of pleasure ran through several octaves, then I too went silent as I just wheezed, almost insensate with the built-up power of this orgasm.

Each pulsing blast of my cock was almost painful as I filled her. Then she bucked, her pussy contracting so hard she pushed me out of her. My wildly potent cock blasted her ass with cum, before sending streamers up her back. She turned, reaching down to stroke my painfully powerful length. I shot long ropes of cum up her body, and she reveled in it, releasing me to smear it over herself, which only made me cover her with more.

So... *this* is why she'd wanted to be in the shower.

I'd covered her, and the walls, and most of myself by the time I'd finished, and I was panting hard, having to hold myself up, propped on a wall.

Ana slid down to her knees, giggling and whispering, "Holy Fuck," over and over again.

Then, those silver eyes looked up at me. "That was so fucking hot... Literally and figuratively. I've wanted to do something like that ever since you destroyed Grey's room in my basement. Just... feel your rush all over me again. Thanks, caveman."

My cock twitched and spurted a bit more onto my leg. I didn't care. I gave a frazzled laugh.

"First my cock was in pain, now my balls are. Gods!" My sack ached, shriveled and tight. "I'm definitely going to need a moment."

She smiled. "Good, that's what I wanted to hear. Can't have you sparing a single drop of love, now can we?"

She rose... or tried to, but I had to help her. She turned the shower on to steaming warmth and we both washed off.

Once she was clean, she whispered, "Join us when you're ready again."

Then she kissed me, winked, and strode powerfully out of the bathroom, still dripping wet and naked.

What a woman!

FEN

A<small>NA</small> <small>STRODE INTO THE LIVING AREA:</small> <small>PROUD, NAKED, WET,</small> and sexy as Hel!

"Your turn," she said, voice husky, beckoning me with a finger.

I was up in an instant, but I didn't rush to her. I wanted to savor this sight, drinking her in as I approached.

"Like what you see?" she asked with a sly smile.

"Hel yes!" I breathed. "I can say with certainty, there is no one like you, my goddess. You are magnificent, extraordinary, bounteous, and beautiful, and you aren't afraid to show it." I knelt before her. "How may I serve you?"

I brought one of her hands to my lips and kissed the back of it softly, my eyes never leaving her silvery gaze.

She shivered, the sensation rolling down her body from her head to her pussy.

"You always have all the right words," she murmured. "I think I know exactly how I want you to... ah... serve me. Come, my love."

I rose and let her lead me into the bedroom. The shower was going in the ensuite, but I ignored that and focused on my beloved, following her halfway to the bed before she turned to me.

She looped her arms around my neck drawing herself up — and my head down — to kiss my lips lightly, brushing her lush, wet body against my clothes.

"I want you to serve me with your lips," she whispered. "Talk to me, use all those wonderful words and tell me everything you feel... while also using your mouth to pleasure me. That's what I want."

Sounded good to me.

But then she hesitated. "Or...do I need to be the one talking to calm your wolf?"

"No," I said softly. This was one of the reasons I wanted to be alone with her. "Something changed when you faced down my wolf in Queens. I don't need to hear your voice anymore, even just thinking about you calms my wolf. You've... changed me. And I want to show you how much I love you and appreciate that, so yes, I'll use my mouth to tell you how wonderful you are and to pleasure you. There's nothing I'd love more."

"Oh... wow... okay, continue." The dark blush on her already flushed cheeks was like dessert for my eyes.

Leaning down, I brushed her lips in a teasing kiss as I put my hands on her hips. Then, sliding my hands up her sides, I caressed the fullness of her breasts before circling my arms around her, pressing her close to me.

I brought my lips to her ear and spoke in a breathy whisper. "Your flesh may be finite, but your heart and soul are boundless and free, and you capture every man who sees you. I've been forever ensnared by you and revel in my imprisonment. I love you, Anais Baker. I have since the moment I saw you, and I will for eternity. Even if I pass from this world, my love will endure."

She shivered and let out a long breathy moan. "Wow, great start. What's next?"

I kissed her cheek, then her rosy lips, savoring their sweetness.

With a low throaty groan, I swept my lips lower, over her chin and neck, her shoulders, and the tops of her breasts. Burying my face in her heavenly cleavage I lingered on a searing, licking kiss. I'd return there eventually, but for now, I sank lower, pressing my lips to her stomach where I found that strange rose tattoo low on her abdomen. I kissed the Celtic knot of a flower, then traced more kisses down the stem to her pubic bone.

A long, soft moan slipped from her lips in anticipation of what would come next, but I waited just a moment, gazing up at her searing, silver eyes. Her hands came to my head, stroking through my long blond hair as she trembled. I darted my tongue out to slash at her pubic bone again, then flicked it lower to brush her clit.

She gasped, but that was only the beginning. I dipped lower, slowly drawing my tongue along her folds. I took my time tasting her honey-lemon sweetness, along with the salty tang of another man's cum. Then I finished with a flick up over her clit before humming my contentment to myself.

Ana blew out a long trembling breath, her hands tightening their grip in my hair. "Yes," she breathed.

"You're so amazingly sweet," I said, kissing that tattoo once again. "It's some miracle of your body, and I love it. I could eat nothing but your pussy and be satisfied." I flicked my tongue out again, retracing its last path, pressing on her slit and clit. Then shuddered with my own contented sigh. "Oh, yeah."

"Enough teasing, get your face in there." She pushed my head closer, but kneeling as I was, I couldn't get the best angle. So, I reached around, grabbed her ripe, round ass, and lifted her carefully, tossing her effortlessly back a few feet, onto the bed.

She yelped and laughed as I rushed to the side of the bed, kneeling and opening her legs to press my lips to her folds, beginning my feast in earnest.

Her hands returned to my hair, nails digging into my scalp as I lashed my tongue over her heavenly mound. Then I slid inside her, in and up, to taste her g-spot.

"Holy fuck!" she cried out. "I love your tongue!"

I kept that up, softly brushing her g-spot while my mouth covered her and I sucked on her clit, carefully brushing my teeth over the sensitive nub.

That... apparently was too much for her.

"Oh gods, yes!" she screamed, and her channel tightened around my tongue as her pussy flooded with sweet juices.

I drank greedily from that heavenly chalice and moaned my own bliss at her divine flavor.

When she was finished, body quivering, I slowly drew my face back, unashamed of her wetness dripping over my chin.

"Feeling your rush and tasting your cum is almost as good as coming myself," I breathed. Indeed, my cock was rock hard and ready even though I was still fully dressed.

"Do you want to get off?" she asked, a little breathless. "You can. You've already given me something wonderful. Your words, your lips, and that... that fucking miracle tongue of yours. I know I'm a goddess, but you make me *feel* like a goddess, Fen."

Good.

"No, I don't need anything," I said, and meant it.

Last night I'd had an amazing time with her *and* she now carried my child.

I could wait to get off.

"When I told the others I wished to have some time with you alone," I said, "it was entirely for this, to worship my goddess and bring you only the most divine pleasure."

"You're so selfless and patient," she breathed with a laugh.

"It's kind of sick," came a gravelly voice.

Ana twitched as I looked at Ramsey standing in the doorway to the ensuite, stroking that monster cock of his.

"Don't mind me," he said with a grin. "This is Fen's time. Keep going. I'm just gonna watch our goddess get off and make sure I'm ready for round two."

"Ramsey, you pervert," Ana said, though her tone was playful, not accusing. Then she rose a little to look down at me. "Is that okay with you?"

I grinned. "I don't need to worship you in private. Let everyone see my devotion and how I praise you."

Ana laughed. "Then, by all means, continue." She fell back on the bed.

"Would my goddess like a show?" I asked as I stood.

"Ooooh, yes!" she said with a giggle. "You gonna strip for me?"

I smiled in answer, taking out my phone and quickly getting to the song I wanted.

The thumping base of Nine Inch Nails' *Closer* thrummed to life, and I threw the phone down on the bed to free my hands. I figured this particular song was perfect to strip to. With me being part wolf, the lyrics seemed appropriate. Not to mention that Ana definitely got me "closer to God."

I danced, slow and swaying, as I unbuttoned my shirt, pulled it open, and slid my hands over my abs, up to my chest.

Ana's hand slid down to stroke her pussy and clit as she watched me with hungry eyes. Gods, that was sexy.

Slowly, I shrugged out of my shirt, continuing to feel myself and sliding my hands up into my long hair to hold there as I shifted and undulated my hips. I'd recently started taking stripper-dance classes just for this purpose.

With her heated, captivated gaze following my hands, I pushed them down my body into my pants and grabbed my junk.

Ana's breathing picked up and she jerked upright.

"I want to see this part close up," she said, voice breathy, as I undid my pants and pushed them down inch by agonizingly slow inch. "If only I had some cash to stuff in your... oh!"

My cock sprang out — I'd gone commando today — and her eyes widened, her words stalling as she sucked in a sharp breath as if she hadn't seen me naked before.

Hot tingles of pleasure burst to life at the base of my spine as the hunger in her eyes grew.

Ana reached out and grabbed my cock. Her gaze tore a path up my body to meet mine as I thrusted into her hand with rocking hips.

The first song ended, and the next began: Robert Palmer's *Simply Irresistible.*

"You sure you don't want something?" Ana asked, squeezing my cock and bringing the tip to her lips, licking off the small pool of pre-come.

I smiled. "Later, when we're all together."

She nodded.

"I'm not done worshiping you with my lips yet."

She laughed. "Then by all means continue."

I kicked off my pants, urged her to lie back, and leaned over her. Pressing my rigid shaft against her pussy,

I rubbed my length over her as I teased my lips over her breasts.

"Oooh, yes," she breathed.

I kissed all over those heavy, round orbs, tracing wet patterns with my long tongue, and when I sucked a hard nipple into my mouth, she moaned, grinding her clit against my cock.

I licked and teased that rock-hard bud, creating a solid hard suction before pulling away, taking her breast with me, making her mewl and shudder.

With a pop, I released her, watching her bosom jiggle and settle back. Then... I did the same on the other side.

Ana moaned and began panting, needful gasps. She pressed her hands to the back of my head, apparently not wanting me to let go this time.

I redoubled my efforts with my tongue and careful teeth on her taut, swollen nipples. Then Ana cried out, her pussy flooding over my balls and her nipple shot several spurts of warm liquid into my mouth.

My eyes went wide, and I would have pulled off her breast in surprise if she hadn't been holding me in place.

Tentatively, I reached my hand up to her other breast and massaged it, tweaking her nipple. It squirted forcibly as well, and Ana gasped and mewled in delight. She writhed through her orgasm, head pushed back into the bed, body shaking and convulsing.

She eventually let my head go, and I cleaned off her nipple with my tongue then moved to the other one, doing the same before sliding to lay beside her.

She wore a beatific grin as she panted heavily, regaining her breath.

"That was new," I whispered.

She laughed, then winked. "Thought you might like that." She had to pause to drink in more air before continuing. "I have... control over my fertility, so I thought... I'd accelerate the production of milk and give you a treat." She gave a breathy laugh. "Also, best nipple-orgasm ever!"

I leaned over to kiss her lips. "I'm glad you liked it. Are you ready for all of us together now?" I asked, my lips moving against hers.

"Oh, gods, yes! I'd forgotten about that," she gasped.

It was good to know my lip service had distracted her that much.

"Thank you, Fen," she murmured before firmly kissing me. "That was amazing. *You're* amazing and so patient. Gods, I just want to make you come so hard."

"I will," I said, my voice dropping an octave into a low growl. "I promise."

She shivered with pleasure. "Then let's do this!"

ANAIS

"Can you get Grey?" Fen asked Ramsey, reminding me the big man was still watching us.

I rolled my head to the side to see Ramsey, still slowly rubbing his massive dick, with a cocky smile on that deeply tanned face.

He winked at me, then shouted, "Grey! Time to fuck!" before pushing himself off from the doorway and strutting over to the bed.

I couldn't help but laugh. I was sure that hadn't been what Fen had wanted, but it was pure Ramsey.

"That's a new bed," Grey said with just a hint of dismay as he hurried into the room and began to undress.

"Don't worry, we haven't destroyed it... yet," I said.

Grey looked around. His bedroom was... expansive, and there was no shortage of space. The question was: where would be comfortable for the four of us to do our thing, if not the bed?

"Any fantasies, you'd like to fulfill?" Fen whispered beside me, his hot breath on my cheek sending an expectant thrill through me.

My horny self hadn't had much to say in a while since I'd been living her dream life, but now... with Fen's question hanging in my mind, she squirmed to life.

There is something I've always wanted to try... and doing it standing up would be an extra level of difficulty. But could be very rewarding!

I giggled as the thought came to life in my head. Oh... yeah... I wanted to try that!

"If the bed's not an option, then... we'll just have to do this standing," I said, slowly slipping toward the edge of the bed to sit. "But... I'm already weak in the knees so someone's going to have to help me up."

Fen was there in an instant, scooping me into his arms as he stood beside the bed. I looped my arms around his neck, even though my arms were pretty weary as well.

"What're you thinking, Silverlocks?" Ramsey asked.

I hadn't heard him get close, but he was suddenly right there beside Fen and I could feel the heat from his large body.

Yup, this was exactly what I was going for.

I reached a hand over to stroke Ramsey's mountainous chest.

"You get to be in my ass again," I whispered. Our gazes locked and his midnight blue eyes shimmered with anticipatory fervor.

"Sounds good to me," he rumbled.

"While Grey and Fen are going to be good little boys and share my pussy."

Grey had finished disrobing and came to join the three of us, laying a hand on my thighs draped over Fen's arm. "I don't mind sharing," he breathed.

But Fen caught on quicker. "At... the same time?" he asked.

I licked my lips and nodded, a shiver thrilling through me just thinking about it.

"Oh..." Grey said. Then a deeper, more heated, "Oooh."

Fen shifted me, carefully and slowly until I was vertical, standing on his feet as the three guys moved in close around me. Their pressing forms kept me standing... because my watery-weak legs weren't going to do the job.

With my arms still around Fen's neck, I brought his lips down to mine for a long, deep kiss, his miracle tongue exploring my mouth. I tasted myself on his lips and had to admit, I was pretty damned sweet.

Then I shifted a little taking one of my arms and reaching around Grey's neck, bringing the two of them in front of me. I switched between their lips as Ramsey's large hands roamed my back and sides, his lips hard on my shoulders and hair.

For a long moment, we lingered in this tight embrace, pressed close and savoring the feel and taste of each other.

Then Ramsey whispered in my ear from behind. "Get your ass ready, Silverlocks. I want to be inside you."

And I wanted him inside me.

I surged my sex aspect to loosen my ass for him as his large hands landed on my butt cheeks, lifting me easily. Then... came the massive, probing tip of his cock knocking on my back door.

"Ready," I whispered to him during a rare moment when my lips weren't occupied by Fen or Grey.

Uncharacteristic for Ramsey, he entered me slowly with soft, shallow thrusts, carefully pushing deeper until my ass cheeks were pressed to his hips.

"Oh, hell yeah," he breathed, his tongue teasing the tip of my ear, sending shudders rolling down my body.

Just the feel of that monster cock stretching my ass was enough to stoke the slowly building flames of new arousal within me to a raging bonfire. My core sizzled with heat, bubbling like lava in a volcano ready to explode.

Next... I gingerly lifted my legs. I slid my left leg up beside Grey and he got the hint, grabbing it and helping me up as I looped it around his waist. Then, spread wide — very close to doing a suspended splits — I did the same with my right leg around Fen and he held me in place as well... although Fen and Grey were hardly needed since Ramsey's powerful cock was practically keeping me aloft as it was.

I felt the twin cocks of Grey and Fen slipping around my inner thighs and lower, under me.

"Fen first, then Grey," I instructed, though I was panting and near to breathless from the slow strokes of Ramsey in my ass, not to mention the intensity of pure manhood which pressed in around me.

Fen dipped down to kiss me softly before he rose again, and his cock slipped through my drenched folds. For a moment he was there, in front, possessing me as he rocked his hips through several long thrusts.

I moaned and shivered, so very close to my peak. But I didn't want to come yet, so I held it back with my aspect. Thrilling heat thrummed through me at the thought of what we were doing, pounding in time with my racing heart.

Then Fen shifted to the side and Grey was there. It was awkward, the two of them needing to be almost face to face. I surged my sex, opening my pussy to allow Grey's probing cock to slip in beside Fen's. My legs were stretched back now, achingly wide, but I knew this position would be worth any residual pain.

Grey slid home, stretching my folds, sheathed tight with Fen, filling me fuller than I'd ever been before, and yet, as uber-stimulating as it was to have these two hunks double stuffed inside me, what really caught my attention was how close Fen and Grey were to each other. Their cheeks brushed, Fen's fair skin against Grey's bronzed tan.

"Kiss," I said to them. "I want you two to kiss."

Fen — glorious, wonderful, always-ready-to-please

Fen — was instantly into it. He brushed his lips by Grey's ... who wasn't into it?

Grey didn't shy away from Fen, though, just seemed stoically stone-faced, his brow furrowed in thought before he came to some kind of conclusion.

"As my goddess wishes," Grey breathed, and he turned his head ever so slightly to meet Fen's lips.

And seeing them open to each other, tongues slipping between those hard manly lips while their two incredible cocks shifted within me. Yeah... that was exactly the fantasy moment I'd been dreaming of, and I gave a guttural cry as I came so hard I nearly pushed all three of them out of me.

I felt like I'd been launched into the clouds, a divine serenity filling my soul, even as my body erupted with an orgasm so powerful, I felt it in my fingertips and toes. I swear, even my hair curled at the extreme sexiness of that moment.

I spewed a litany of wordless praises as I writhed and shook, held firm between my three phenomenal guys.

Ramsey chuckled behind me. "Damn girl, we're only getting started!"

I couldn't speak, so I laughed into Ramsey's soul. *Then I think it's time you blew my mind, don't you?*

Hell, yeah! he whispered back, and his soft, slow thrusts turned to rapid, hard, slamming lunges.

Yes! More! I soul-whispered to Fen and Grey. I didn't know what to say exactly. I just knew I wanted them to join Ramsey in letting loose in this moment, no holding back. I wanted to feel all three of my guys giving me everything they had!

My heart seemed to swell and thrash against the inside of my chest, my breathing turning ragged and wheezing. I knew I could use my sex aspect to regain control of myself, but I didn't want to. I wanted to feel every glorious moment of this. I was already sky-high with bliss, but I knew these three could send me into deep space if they wanted to.

And they did.

It took an awkward moment for Fen and Grey to find their rhythm, alternating thrusts into my — very receptive and flooded — pussy.

The three of them sensed the impending culmination of this amazing moment and pressed closer still. Grey's and Fen's faces came to mine, in a strange three-way kiss. Fen's supernatural tongue alternated between my mouth and Grey's as the three of us tried to devour each other. And behind, Ramsey's lips were hard on the back of my head and shoulders.

Fen's arms stretched around Ramsey and Grey, pulling us all in closer, while Grey did the same and Ramsey supported me, his hands curled under my thighs, pulling them back as wide as they would go.

My already raging orgasm redoubled in bliss, then doubled again. I'd already been pleasured beyond reason. All I wanted now was for this miraculous moment to find its ultimate fulfillment.

I... I love you all. This is perfect... Perfect! I called into their souls at the same time. Then, I surged my love and sex simultaneously into all three of them, filling their entire bodies with my devotion... and a visceral need to release.

All three men cried out as one, bodies rippling with orgasmic bliss. Three inhuman explosions filled me, and the rush of those mutually powerful releases shot me into the depths of purest ecstasy with such intensity I blacked out.

Again, I had an out-of-body experience. My soul shivered as I watched the clump of us twitching and grunting, crammed so tightly together. The heavenly hard muscles on three manly frames bunched and rippled as they crushed around me and into each other.

It was a moment of true joining, as close as our bodies could get, while our souls merged and quivered in a union of desire and love.

I let out a delicious sigh, then was shot back into my body... writhing in perfect euphoria.

SOMETIME LATER, I LOUNGED ON THE BED AGAIN. GREY FED me grapes, while Fen cleaned the floor where the four of us had been. Yeah... we'd all been... overflowing... with our desires. Ramsey was just getting out of the shower, and he sauntered into the bedroom as Fen rose, done with his duties, and the two of them joined Grey on the bed with me.

"We may come and go on our own," Fen said. "But this will probably be our last night together for a while."

I sighed, both grateful and sad. "That was perfect. A perfect moment. Thank you, all of you. I cherish every moment with each of you, but I'm a little sad we won't be doing *that* again for a while."

"Yeah, me too," Ramsey said softly. I think we were all surprised to hear that. Of all my guys, Ramsey was the one who most resisted this strange foursome of ours.

"Oh?" I prompted.

Ramsey took a long time before he spoke, looking everywhere but at the three of us. Then... apparently, he decided the manly thing was to just say how he felt.

"I love you, Ana," he said, his words coming out in a rush, "and I don't fucking care who knows it or who else loves you. I can't live without you, and I... I want you to have all the love in the world. I love you... and I love everyone you love because they love you too. I don't know if that makes sense, but fuck it, that's how I feel." It came out almost like a challenge.

"Thank you, Ramsey," I whispered.

Not that long ago, I would have struggled to accept someone's love like that. Harder still would have been admitting my own love. Perhaps it was knowing who my mother was or just... the amount of support and dedication these guys had shown me, but I was starting to feel a lot freer with my emotions.

"I love you, too," I replied. "I love all of you."

"Loving Ana is just a given," Fen said easily. "Anyone

who doesn't love her must be incapable of feeling a damned thing. I love you, Ana. And I love you, Ramsey, big lug that you are." Then he whispered to Grey, "And you're a great kisser."

"Yeah, I know," Grey said, as if it were nothing. Then he turned to me. "I love you, and I'll always be there for you, no matter what you need. And..." He drew in a long breath, side-eyeing Fen and Ramsey. "If loving you means loving these oafs, I guess I can handle that."

That was probably as good as I was going to get from these three.

"You guys are... just... wow," I whispered, feeling a wave of drowsiness take me. I felt so contented and sated and loved and relaxed. "Stay with me tonight?" I asked. "After that, I'll see you when I see you."

There was some shifting after that as we all moved under the covers, Fen behind Grey on one side and Ramsey on the other. Like they had before, they pressed close. I wouldn't have much room to move while sleeping, but I didn't care. Their heat and the muscled press of their bodies did wonders to relax me into the best sleep I'd had since... last night.

ANAIS

I was so well rested and happy the next day, I couldn't help but laugh freely and hum to myself as I puttered around Grey's penthouse. I was on cloud nine... or perhaps even cloud ten or eleven? Was there a cloud one hundred? If so, I was there.

Grey was out. He'd said he had some things to attend to for his business. Mostly, he wasn't running things anymore, but a few things still needed his attention as he tried to divest himself of those companies.

Caia was doing some early Christmas shopping, and Eva was out with Trent, which left me and Reia at the penthouse.

"You really are out of it, aren't you, Mom?" Reia asked as she sat on the high chair across the breakfast bar opposite me, folding her hands on the countertop, prim and proper.

Pulled from my heavenly reverie, I blinked at her. "Hmmm? Oh? Why do you say that?"

"You're eating sour cream straight from the container."

She gave the container a pointed look, and I stopped mid motion with a spoonful on its way to my mouth.

"I... isn't this yogurt?" I checked the container.

Nope. Not yogurt. Swell.

"Yup, completely out of it." I put the sour cream back in the fridge and sighed, still contentedly happy. "Did you need something?"

I glanced back at her, the fridge still open, knowing my meaning could be taken two ways, but Reia shook her head.

"It's the weekend so I have no homework... which means I'm free. But I also don't have many hobbies." Her gaze darted around the room as if she were looking for something to do. "I used to play chess with Uncle Donny, but now he's away on business a lot."

Reia had taught me how to play chess, but I was still horrible, so I didn't suggest we play.

"I was actually coming to see if *you* needed *me* for anything?" Her tone suggested I did, and she seemed desperate to be tasked with something.

The poor girl didn't know how to have fun... which reminded me.

"How was the club last night? Any cute boys hit on you?" I wiggled my eyebrows suggestively. Then I ducked into the fridge and this time made sure I grabbed the yogurt. When I came back to the breakfast bar, Reia was giving me a sour look.

"Mom... I'm sixteen. Do you really want twenty-something men hitting on me?"

I blinked. No, probably not. But that got me thinking. If she was only sixteen, then... "How did you get into the club?"

"The guy checking IDs took one look at Caia, fell madly in love with her, and mostly ignored me."

"So..." Did I really want to ask this question. I scooped up a mouthful of yogurt, then decided I'd rather know than not know. It was Reia after all. "What *did* you do?"

"I tried a rum and coke, but I didn't like it. After that, I drank club soda and watched all the silly people trying desperately to hook up."

Which sounded exactly like Reia.

"And how did Caia get along?" I asked, although, I had a feeling I knew.

"Guys bought her drinks, like... too many. She had a table full of drinks, most of which she didn't try. She watched the silly people too and we chatted a lot, catching up. She thinks I should try for Harvard Law School."

Reia did have my aspect of law, so... yeah, I could see that. She was also incredibly smart like Caia, and Harvard wouldn't be out of reach.

"Do you want that?"

"Don't know yet. Maybe?" She was agitated, uncertain, which wasn't like her. She hopped off her stool and got a spoon out of the kitchen drawer, returning to dip into the yogurt with me.

I couldn't think of anything to ask after that, so silence reigned awkwardly as we each took turns eating spoonfuls of yogurt

Then Reia asked, "Mom... what do *you* want?"

I blinked, spoon poised mid-dunk. "What?"

"What do you want?" she repeated. "Out of life. I... I get that you're a goddess now, which is odd, but still, don't goddesses want things? You've seemed different these past few weeks, like you're really trying to figure yourself out, which is great. So, I was curious if you know what you want."

Oh, my dear, darling girl, always being the adult in our relationship.

I smiled. "I love you, Reia. Thank you for noticing how I've been changing. As for what I want... I don't know yet."

I want more stunning sex with my gorgeous guys.

Yeah, I wasn't going to say that out loud. But was there more beyond that...?

That reminded me of my little journal and my 'I AM' list.

"Oh! You want to help, Reia?" I asked, hopping up, and grabbing my little notebook from my purse. "You can help me figure out more about myself. Would you like that?"

She beamed. "Yes! What do you need?"

"I have this list of traits, but I'm trying to expand it to see if anything really sinks in. That might help me figure out what I want."

I sat in the chair beside her, opened up my notebook, and read off my list. So far, it included: a mother, a lover, beautiful, charismatic, a helper (a bartender), a healer, a fighter for justice — oh... I'd forgotten I'd written that one down, it made a lot more sense now — but that was the end of my list. I quickly added: *a warrior*.

"Well, what do you think?" I asked Reia.

"You're kind and gentle," Reia said quickly. I jotted that down. "I don't know if it's the same as being... a lover —" she blushed furiously, "—but you have a large heart, Mom."

"Thank you," I said, noting that.

"Would you ever want to help the homeless or less fortunate?" Reia suggested.

"Maybe?" Honestly, that didn't feel quite right for me. I was a bit too much of a prissy princess for that.

I gave a huff and reluctantly added *prissy princess* to my list. Not everything on the list needed to be things I liked about myself. Still, there was something about the idea of helping the less fortunate.

"I... *do* want to help people... and I *am* a goddess. Aren't gods supposed to listen to their worshipers and answer prayers or something?" My mind made a leap, and suddenly I had an idea. "Oh, oh!" I said, clapping. "I want to help people with love... and maybe to have better sex. Because bad sex is just awful. Maybe I could be some sex guru or matchmaker. A love sage. Is that a thing?"

Reia was blushing again. "Uh... I wouldn't know about the bad sex part."

Without thinking, I said, "I'm pretty sure you've masturbated before. Isn't it awful when you're really horny but you can't seem to get off?"

She stared at me wide-eyed and I blinked.

Yep... I'd just said that to my sixteen-year-old daughter.

Then her face went a deep crimson and her eyes grew comically wide. She swallowed hard, and a strangled sound escaped her lips.

"Ah... well... I guess if I was going to talk about that to anyone... you *are* a sex goddess, so you'd know, right?" she said, then hesitated.

Her mouth moved, but only breathy little sounds came out as she struggled with what she was trying to say. I stayed silent and let her have the space to figure it out.

Eventually, in a hushed voice, she asked, "What is good sex like?"

I beamed. Finally! My daughter had asked me about something I was an expert on.

"Well..." Thoughts of last night flashed through my mind... but that probably wasn't realistic and if I was going to take this seriously, I needed to be careful not to go overboard and embarrass her too much. "What's your favorite sweet, sinful dessert or food?"

If I knew my daughter at all, she'd say cheesecake. There was a vegan recipe she used which she swore was better than regular cheesecake.

Reia thought for a second, then replied, "Raspberry cheesecake. The sweetness of the raspberries with the smooth and silky texture of the cheesecake is heavenly." She gave a contented smile and sighed.

"Now, imagine that, only ten times as pleasurable. Also, it's filling your entire body, not just your mouth... Well, it could be filling your mouth... but... ah... yeah, ignore that. It makes you shake and shiver with delight and you never want it to end. I'd say that's good sex."

"Oh... wow... really?"

"Yup." But I figured there was a fairly large proviso that went with this. "*But...* most guys, especially ones at your age, and even some older ones, aren't as concerned about blowing their partner's mind as they are with blowing their... ah... their own minds."

Reia grimaced. "Yeah, exactly! How can a girl find a good guy?"

I sighed. "Well, I was horrible at that for a very long time. But I can say a few things with certainty that I wished I'd realized when I was your age. First, don't just date a guy because he's hot and he says a few nice things to you. It's easy enough for any guy to fake being nice just to get into your pants."

She nodded and her fingers twitched as if she wanted a pen so she could take notes.

"More than what they say, notice what they do, how they treat you and others. They need to... ah... well, they need to worship you. Oh, and it may seem obvious to you, but there is a huge difference between sex and love. A guy can give you great, mind-blowing sex and still not love you. In summary: any guy can say he loves you, but it's only the special ones who show it in everything they do, who respect you enough to treat you like a... well, a goddess."

Reia nodded. "Sounds pretty fucking rare."

"It is. Which is what makes love so special when you find it. Talk to Eva and Trent sometime. I think they've finally found their match. They might have some insights."

"And... what do I do until I find the right guy?" she asked a bit sheepishly. At least she wasn't blushing so deeply anymore.

"You have a couple options. Vibrators are your friend. I have a whole bunch you can try—"

"Mom!" Reia was instantly beet-red again.

"What? Most of them I haven't even used. And good cleaning is a must for sex toys, so...yeah." I sighed, knowing I'd pushed the limit for her right now. "If that's not your thing, you can just go ahead and experiment with guys."

Reia scrunched up her nose. "Like have random sex with some guy?"

"Not *some* guy. A guy who *you've* chosen who strikes your fancy. It doesn't have to be forever. You can just date and have some fun. Just make sure you're on the pill and they're using condoms."

I stood and put the yogurt back in the fridge and our spoons in the sink. "That's actually a good gauge of asshole versus not asshole. If they're willing to wear a condom for you, that's one step toward respect. Also, if you're going the fun route, don't commit too much of your heart. Just... have some fun and see what you like. Don't be afraid to ask for what you want. Trial and error isn't perfect, but it helped me figure out what I liked and didn't. Just... like I said... be careful."

Reia nodded.

"If neither of those options appeal," I added, "well, your fingers can still be quite stimulating. As with the other options, practice makes perfect."

Reia kept nodding. "Maybe, I'll stick with that for now."

We sat in silence for a long moment before Reia asked, "Did that help you figure out anything?"

That was Reia for you, deftly turning the whole conversation around, back to where we'd started: my life goals.

"Hunh... I think it might have, yes," I said. "I think I might want to help the less fortunate... but specifically those who are less fortunate in love. I could be a sex-ed teacher, or love-life coach, or..." Another idea occurred to me which I *loved*. "I could help women get out of bad relationships and into good ones, or even just help them love themselves and move on from there. I can use my war aspect to deal with the dickhead men in their lives, then help them find a new path and hopefully true love in the process!" Something about that really seemed to hit home for me.

Reia smiled. "Sounds like you're excited about that."

"I... think I am. Though I have no clue how to do any of that."

Reia laughed. "You'll figure it out. If there's one thing we Baker women do well, it's striving toward our goals and achieving them."

That was very true.

Baker women...

Something about that reminded me... "Oh, hey, I should tell you. You're going to be a sister all over again... to triplets."

Reia's brilliant blue eyes went wide. "Again? More kids?"

I shrugged. "I'm a fertility goddess... so... yeah. After this, I think I'll be done, but... I really wanted to be a mother — to babies — again. And Grey, Ramsey, and Fen have all promised to help out. I don't think I could deal with three kids without my guys around."

Reia shook her head. "Your choice, I guess."

It was. And that reminded me I had wanted to call Freyja to find out more about my fertility and what I could do with it.

"If you'll excuse me," I said, rising and heading to the downstairs lounge for privacy. "I... need to make a call."

ANAIS

"Hi, Freyja!" I said into my phone. "It's Anais Baker. You helped my uncle remember who he was. Remember me?"

There was an audible sigh from the other end of the line as I paced the length of the downstairs lounge, phone pressed to my ear. I was both concerned and excited about what might be possible with my fertility aspect.

Freyja, though, seemed less than excited to hear from me. "Hello, Anais. Yes, I remember you. What time is it?"

I blinked at the odd question, then quickly checked my phone. "Ah... it's eleven thirty."

"A.M.?" she hissed.

"Yes?"

"Fuck me." Freyja groaned.

Had I gotten her up? "Ah... sorry if I woke you?" I said

apologetically, turning and making another lap to the far end of the lounge.

"Well, too late now. The damage is done," she huffed. "Why are you calling?"

Now I felt selfish and inane for asking, but... I wasn't going to hang up and try calling again. She might never answer or she just might block me. As she said, the damage was already done, I'd just have to suck it up and accept that I'd pissed off another goddess.

"I wanted to know more about the aspect of fertility," I said. "It seems I also have that aspect and... I'm pregnant. So, I'm wondering... what's possible?"

"You called me, in the middle of *my* night, for that? Didn't that beautiful sort-of grandson of mine tell you I was a night owl?"

I did recall mention of Freyja being a *bad girl* and something about *infidelity*, but nothing about being a night owl. "No, sorry. I can call back later if—"

"No." Another sigh. "Just... no, it's fine. Like I said, damage is done. You want to know about fertility? You're pregnant?"

"Yup."

"Well, if you don't want the kid, just get rid of it," she said. "You can cause your own miscarriages and the earlier the better."

"Oh." That seemed awful.

I turned to stare out the windows at the Manhattan skyline as the wind whipped up leaves from the many trees below and scattered them around the city.

"Better yet, do what I do and just switch off that annoying aspect altogether. I mean my first hundred kids were nice, but after that... I lost count and just didn't care anymore."

First... hundred?

Fuck me!

"Ah... okay. Good to know. I may do that after I've had these kids. But for now, I'm more wondering what I can do around the pregnancy itself."

"*These kids?* How many are you having?"

"Three, triplets."

"Fuck, girl! Why would you do that to yourself?"

"I... I..." I didn't feel like explaining that I'd wanted one kid from each of my guys. That was none of her business. "I have, and I don't want to undo it. So, is there anything I can do? I have three daughters already. I had them before I had the aspect of fertility, so I know what a regular pregnancy is like. Is there a way to avoid all that pain and discomfort?"

"Wait, what?" she gasped. "You had three kids *before* you had this aspect? How did that work?"

Right, most gods and goddesses had their aspects all their lives. I was different, special for some reason, and I had no clue why my aspects had shown up later in life. It was yet another thing I'd have to ask my dad... if I ever found him.

"I'm strange," I said, hoping she wouldn't want more of an explanation.

"Yeah, you are..." She paused and I heard something

rustling in the background. "What... is regular pregnancy like?"

I blinked. She didn't know? Well, that spoke volumes about what might be possible with this aspect.

"Why don't you tell me what your pregnancies were like?" I asked. "That will give me a sense for what's possible and then I can tell you how a regular pregnancy is different."

Freyja sighed. "Ah... well... I get knocked up, then I pop the kid out."

I waited for more. When it didn't come, I asked, "And how long did that process take?" She made it sound like a relatively quick affair.

"For the first few, I let it take a while, a few days, just to feel the life growing inside me. But after the first dozen or so, I gave up on that and just had them right away."

Wait, what?

A few DAYS!

Right away?

"When you say, 'right away,' you mean... like instantly after conception?"

"Pretty much. My brother used to call it 'blowing up the balloon.' I once had three kids in one night with the same god."

"Oh..." I said and my brain stalled out on the one word, repeating it over and over again in my mind.

Oh, indeed.

I shook myself out of my stupor. "Ah, well, regular pregnancy is quite a bit different. It takes nine months or so, and it can be rather strenuous and painful, but also rewarding at the same time."

"Nine fucking months?" she gasped. "How do humans do it?"

"Because for us... ah... I mean them... there isn't any other option if they want to have a child."

"Oh, yeah, right. Well, that sounds like Hel. No wonder you're wondering what's possible. So, first off, yeah, you can pop those puppies out whenever you want, just make it happen. Hel, you don't even have to have them physically. You can just manifest a kid. Aphrodite was born when Uranus masturbated into the ocean, although I hear they're telling that tale differently these days. So, yeah, anyway, you can just will those kids out of you."

That was rather incredible and mind-blowing. But then... that did sound like godly power.

"Though, if you wanted to carry the suckers for a while, you could," she added. "It should be effortless and painless now that you can control fertility. Any and all parts of pregnancy fall into the fertility aspect, so yeah, just... do what you want basically."

That... made sense. I'd been able to produce milk for Fen last night, which was far earlier than should have been possible.

Curious... I concentrated on my fertility aspect for a moment. My breasts had grown during my previous pregnancies, so... I tried to make them get bigger right now. They swelled, painfully large against my — now very restrictive — bra, and I quickly undid the change with an awed smile.

Oh... the guys were going to *love* that. I didn't particularly want my tits to be that much bigger, I liked my size, but knowing I *could* make them bigger or potentially even smaller on a whim... that was something.

"You still there, girl?" Freyja asked.

"Ah... yeah, just experimenting with something."

"Made your tits bigger, did you? Yeah, all the gods *love* that." She didn't sound impressed. I didn't know why I blushed, but I did. "Anything else you need?"

"Ah... no, I think I'm good for now," I replied. "But... if I did want to call and get more advice, when would be a good time?"

"I'm usually up at around two or three."

"In the afternoon?" I confirmed.

"Yeah."

"Thanks, I'll try not to wake you again. Sorry for that, and thanks again for the advice."

I could hear the confused yet motherly tone on the other end. "I don't know why you're needing to ask about this, but... yeah, sure, I'm here if you need anything, girl."

"Thanks again, bye."

"Ciao, bella!" She hung up.

I put my phone away and sat on a couch, sighing heavily.

So... anything was possible...

...because I was a goddess.

That was a lot to take in. Still, it was good to know.

With everything the guys were going through in preparation for this conclave thingy, now probably wasn't the best time to have these kids. But after that, perhaps I'd... *pop them out* as Freyja would say.

"Wow, if only I'd been able to do that before," I whispered to myself.

I'd have to think about it for a while. As it was, I knew my breasts would probably start to get sensitive soon and I didn't know if I wanted that. But again, I could probably turn that on and off, as well.

I shook my head. The possibilities were... astounding.

The door upstairs opened and closed, and I got up and made my way to the main floor to find Grey had returned.

He took one look at me and asked, "What's wrong? You look... rattled. What happened?"

I smiled, though I think it still must have come across as a bit forced. "Ah... just had a chat with Freyja about pregnancy. Still assimilating all of it."

"Ah. Yeah." He quickly ducked in to give me a soft kiss on the cheek. "You need some time alone with that?"

"No. I'm good," I said, grateful he offered. "I could help you with your void this afternoon."

He smiled. "So considerate and thoughtful. I love you, Ana."

The way he said *those three words* so casually almost threw me. But then my heart swelled, my body tingling with pleasant warmth, because it meant his love was ingrained in him now, a part of him.

I drew him down for a long, sensuous kiss, then let him go and spun on my heel, humming as I went to the kitchen to work on lunch. Grey followed — he was a far better cook than I was — and we worked together to prepare a hearty soup and light sandwiches. Reia seemed to sense something was going on and ate quickly before returning to her room.

After lunch, Grey and I went to his office on the lower level.

"Any thoughts on how to do this?" he asked, motioning to his eyes.

The void swirling there didn't pull me in anymore. I was stronger now, a full goddess, and his powers didn't affect me as much.

"You did manage to get it to return when I thought that wasn't possible." He gave a bit of a silly grin — which was very odd for stoic and serious Grey — as he eyed me.

I guessed he was remembering the little seduction act I'd done, draping myself over Ramsey and letting the big man play with me in front of Grey until his void had burned to possess me.

I gave a little laugh. "I don't think sex is going to work this time. I was thinking of using my aspect of love, even though I'm still less familiar with that. It seems to allow me to connect with people's souls... so maybe?"

He nodded. "Worth a try. How do you want me?"

"Crushed against me, with your cock throbbing inside me..." I flashed him a wicked smile. "But we'll save that for a reward once we've done this. Consider it incentive."

He gave a feral grin. "Consider me incentivized."

We worked all afternoon. I spent a lot of time connecting to Grey's soul and trying to help him find peace and control.

It was a struggle at first, but by the end of the afternoon, we were starting to find a rhythm to the work. Grey still wasn't able to turn off his void, but he did seem able to control it more, dimming its influence then surging it again.

After four straight hours, we figured that was a solid day's work. Hopefully, with that as a starting point, he could learn how to turn it off and on as he desired.

Then we showered together, and I showed him how I could make my breasts bigger. It was a very long, and very loud, shower. Reia, who'd been the only one at home that afternoon, couldn't look either of us in the eye at supper.

Caia, Eva, Trent, and Harmonia also joined us for dinner, and we spent a pleasant evening together, but I felt Ramsey and Fen's absence keenly, my heart constricting when I thought of them.

I sent them love, wherever they were, and hoped they could join me again soon.

RAMSEY

THE CONCLAVE WAS IN THREE DAYS, AND IN THE LAST TWO weeks, I'd seen Ana only a few times. Luckily, when I had been free, Grey had stepped away, so I had time alone with her, and once I'd spent myself, I would lay with her, holding her and whispering my love to her. I knew I wasn't as poetic as Fen, but I didn't care. I'd always been straightforward, and I figured that would work too. Ana didn't seem to mind. She was... perfect.

My goddess was everything I needed when I needed it. When all I wanted was to fuck, she was hot and willing and needful. Yet, she could also be a temptress — a vixen — when I wished to be dominated, restrained, and teased with pleasuring pain. If I just needed comfort, she was soft and warm and loving. She was so giving and rarely asked for anything in return. Though, when I'd said as much, she'd only giggled and told me I gave her everything she needed... and more.

It was strange. Being away from her now was both far more agonizing than when I'd first known her... and also far less strenuous. My chaos didn't erupt just because I wasn't around her and was mostly under control now, and my times with her seemed to last me for days of relative peace and quiet.

The new agony I felt was something far deeper. My heart ached when I wasn't with her. But, at the same time, it was also easy to recall pleasant times with her and have that ache soothed.

Was this what true love felt like?

I'd never felt anything like this before and... I was addicted.

Which meant I was probably sporting an odd, sad smile when I arrived at Osiris' office and let myself in without knocking. I knew that would piss off the demanding god, although I was very surprised to find my father, Set, in the room with him.

"Sit," Set said, pointing to a chair.

These two rarely saw eye to eye on anything, so if both of them wanted to see me for something, it had to be important.

"The conclave is just around the corner," Osiris said. "We've discussed it and decided, we have a special task for you."

Oh? That was curious. Usually, I was left alone. I didn't much care for these conclaves and skipped them. Even when they were local and I had a hand in helping set things up, I still bailed on the actual event itself. It was just a bunch of stuck-up gods trying to one-up each other, or rehashing centuries-old feuds.

"Yes?" I asked.

Set cracked a grin, and not a pleasant one. That... didn't bode well.

Osiris nodded. "We want you to handle Horus."

Fuck me. "No, you can't be—"

"Shut up, boy!" Set reprimanded, and I snapped my mouth shut.

If there was one god I truly feared... it was my father. I didn't lose many fights to other daemons, even to other gods, but against him, things were reversed. I'd rarely won a fight against him.

"Listen to your elders and obey," Set said, his tone leaving no room for debate.

I gritted my teeth as Osiris went on. "Usually I'd do it, or Isis would, though she dotes on him a bit too much. I've got other duties this year, and Isis will be helping me. After us, it would fall to Hathor, but it seems she and Horus are on the outs at the moment. She may be his wife and the goddess of love, but even she can only take so much of his bullshit and sleeping around." Osiris sighed.

This was the problem with Horus. He should have been a shining beacon of leadership, a standard for what rulers should be. Instead, he was — as many rulers actually were — selfish, vain, lecherous, and completely self-absorbed. He didn't care for anyone other than himself, except inasmuch as others could serve his every whim.

"Anubis, dedicated son that he is, would usually handle Horus, but he's still dealing with the fallout from that Nari debacle on Samhain. Too many dead whose hearts need weighing and all that. Of the remaining gods, they're either too powerful for me to command or not powerful enough to resist Horus' command compulsions," Osiris said. "That leaves you."

I grunted with a resigned nod. Osiris was right. I could resist Horus, and I definitely *would* resist Horus. But that... was also the problem.

"I'm assuming I don't have permission to kill him if he's being a dick?" I asked. "I promise I'd only kill him a little. Anubis would kick him right back out anyway."

Set laughed.

Osiris sighed. "Look, we know he's a pain, but please refrain from killing him. It's such a nuisance to have to go to the underworld and get his soul back."

That almost made me want to do it more. But still...

"Fine. No killing," I huffed. "Can I lock him in a room and leave him there?"

"No," Osiris said with a hard look. "You're to make him feel at home while he's here and keep him from getting into too much trouble. Restrain his desires for the duration of the conclave, and, for A'aru's sake, keep him away from Zeus and Amaterasu. Most of the other rulership gods are less fussy and willing to just ignore him, but you know how those three can get at each other's throats."

I did.

Horus had had a fling with Amaterasu a while back. Their breakup hadn't been pretty and had nearly ended the world. She was just as vindictive as he was and, in her case, she had every right to be. She'd found him with two other goddesses in the sacred baths, one of whom was her sister.

As for Zeus, he was a well know lech and all-around asshole. He and Horus always butted heads. It wouldn't be easy keeping Horus away from them since all of them would want to assert their divine right of leadership over the conclave. But apparently, I was the shmuck who got to *try* this time around.

I sighed. "I'll do what I can. When is he getting into town?"

"Tomorrow, first thing."

I repeated, "I'll... do what I can. But you know him, so... no promises."

Osiris accepted this with a heavy nod. "I know."

"Anything else?"

Osiris shook his head.

"I'll walk you out," Set said and motioned for me to leave.

Once we were out of Osiris' office, my father shook his head.

"I heard about you losing control. Does it have anything to do with this new goddess you're seeing? If so, dump her and move on. I can't have a son of mine being so reckless. Control your Strife or I'll control it for you... and you won't like that."

I was sure I wouldn't.

"Ana isn't the cause," I said, probably just a bit too aggressively. "Being away from her is what brought out my chaos, but only at first. I'm doing better now. I love her, father, and—"

Set barked a harsh and derisive laugh.

"Love?" He smacked me on the back of the head, sending me hurtling forward, but I managed to catch myself and stagger a few steps instead of falling. "What's gotten into you boy? You weren't made for love. Strife and love don't mix. You really have lost it, haven't you? End it with her, or I will."

Set strode away after that, which was good, as I'd been about to punch him and that probably wouldn't have ended well for me.

There was no way I'd ever end things with Ana. She was my very heart and soul. I'd die without her.

My chaos roiled for a moment, threatening to break free, but I quickly suppressed it.

I was certain that if anything ever happened to Ana, I'd completely lose my mind. I'd be consumed with chaos, lost to it, and I'd go on a rampage... and so would Fen for that matter.

If Set ever tried to do anything to Ana, I knew I'd defend her with everything I had, every fiber of my being. Perhaps then, with something to fight for, I'd finally be able to win against my father.

I MET HORUS AT THE AIRPORT THE NEXT MORNING WITH the longest stretch-limo I could find. He was already in a foul mood, having been banned from yet another airline for assaulting the stewardesses, and the entire ride to the hotel — The Pierre, at the southeast end of Central Park — he babbled about the good old days when women flaunted themselves willingly before him. He demanded I find him some "willing women," and I tried not to vomit as I explained consent to him and how human women would have trouble resisting his godly power and hence, wouldn't be consenting.

Of course, that only made him more furious.

I got him settled into his suite where a functionary from the conclave — I didn't envy the poor lesser daemon who had to serve Horus — came to see to Horus' needs, and Horus listed off his demands, calming down after that.

When I tried to leave, he called after me. "Where are you going, cousin? Are you not going to serve me?" he asked in a petulant and superior tone.

Was there a way I could appease him and still get away from him?

"Ah… yes, of course. I'm here for anything you should need, outside of conclave business, for which you have that other daemon. But you are set in the hotel, and I've ordered up a feast for you. However, I also have other duties I need to attend to as one of the host daemons this year."

"Oh? Duties more important than attending to me?"

Hell, yes! "Equally as important."

He had trouble arguing with that and I made a break for the door.

My hand was on the latch when he called, "Rumor has it you're seeing some new goddess. Is she beautiful?"

I froze. *Fuck!*

I didn't have to look to know there would be a mischievous gleam in his eyes. He just assumed that any goddess seeing another god would swoon for him as soon as she met him, and I had no clue how to answer him.

"I'm hosting a party tomorrow in one of the ball-rooms," he continued, saving me from having to respond. "You should introduce me to this goddess."

Yeah, like hell.

His tone was very suggestive when he said, "I'd very much like to meet her."

That was *not* going to happen.

But as I finally left and made my way home, a cold dread, like a massive stone, formed in my gut. Something told me this conclave was not going to go well.

ANAIS

I answered the knock at Grey's penthouse door to find a man in a suit. He had well-tanned skin, like Ramsey, but he was thin and lithe. His dark hair was cropped close to his head, and he had a cocky grin as he winked an amber-colored eye at me.

"Hey there," he said with a strange drawl. I didn't recognize the accent. "You wouldn't happen to be Anais Baker, the goddess who saved Queens, would you?"

"Ah... yes?" I replied before it occurred to me that perhaps I shouldn't be telling strangers who I was. Though, my daemon sense was telling me this man was an Empyrean, so, at least I hadn't just admitted I was indeed a goddess to a human.

"Great!" he said and pulled out an envelope. "This is for you."

I blinked. Should I take it? I couldn't see any reason not to.

I plucked the pristine golden paper from his hand and looked down at it. In immaculate calligraphy was written: *To Anais Baker*.

When I looked up, the daemon... was gone.

I blinked.

I hadn't heard him leave. He'd just... vanished.

"What the...?"

If it wasn't for the envelope in my hand, I might have thought I'd imagined the whole encounter.

Exceedingly curious now, I opened the envelope. Inside was thick cardstock, the type used for wedding invitations and the like. I pulled it out and read:

*You are among the fortunate and favored
who have been invited by Horus, God of Rulers,
to a most excellent ball.
The Pierre Hotel ~ 2 E 61st St off 5ᵗʰ Avenue
Please arrive at or before 8 pm November 16ᵗʰ
Formal attire required.*

"Huh," I muttered.

"What is it?" Ramsey's voice carried to me.

I looked up and saw him striding out from the elevator.

"An invitation," I said, still a bit stunned.

Ramsey's cheery grin instantly vanished.

"No... he couldn't have... not this quickly!" He hurried to me and plucked the card from my hand, reading it. "Fuck me!" he hissed. "He... he had to have known who you were and... and..." He turned to me. "Did you see who delivered it?" Ramsey asked.

"Yes, a—"

"Slender man, short hair, dark skin like me with a grin that makes you think he knows things about you?"

Ramsey's description was on the money. "Yes."

"Nemty."

"Who?"

"Egyptian daemon messenger, can zip from place to place faster than almost any other god, and one of Horus' lackeys." Ramsey shook his head. "That bastard."

"Nemty?"

"No, Horus."

"Oh." I was lost. "Perhaps we can step inside and you can explain everything to me?" I got the feeling something was happening beyond just an invitation to a ball.

Ramsey gave his trademark grunt, and we went in together.

"So... Horus?" I asked as we headed for the sitting area.

Reia happened to be passing by, heading from the kitchen back to her room with a snack, and she answered me before Ramsey could.

"Egyptian god of rulership, son of Osiris and Isis..." She stopped. "Wait... do you know him?"

"No, but he invited me to a party tomorrow night," I told her.

"I do," Ramsey said. "And he's a right royal ass."

"Oh, curious," Reia said with a tilt of her head... then kept going to her room.

"A ball? Sounds swanky. Are you gonna go?" Eva asked. She was sitting in the TV lounge portion of the large living area, filling out some paperwork for her schooling.

"I don't know," I said.

At the same time Ramsey growled, "No!"

Wow. Controlling much?

Something was up with Ramsey. "Perhaps you should tell me everything." I led him to the main sitting area of the living room and drew him down onto one of the couches next to me.

"Not much to know, other than Horus is a lecherous bastard, who wants to take what belongs to me. Well, I don't think you belong to me, but he does. You get the point."

"Oh," I said, surprised. I tossed the invitation onto the coffee table. "Okay."

If Ramsey said to stay away, I trusted him.

"Although," Ramsey said begrudgingly. "If you don't go..." He sighed and rubbed his face with a large hand. "Horus might get even more vindictive and petulant. I don't think he'd come after you personally, but... you never know with him."

That didn't sound good. "How powerful a god is he?"

Ramsey laughed. "He's not a god at all, despite what he says. He's a daemon prince like me, with aspects of rulership and the heavens. He often tries to claim other aspects, but it's all bluster. He's petty and vindictive and an all-around jerk."

I sighed. "Well then, let him come after me. I'm a goddess with many more aspects, including war. I can take care of myself."

"Yeah, you can," he said with a half laugh, seeming to relax at that. "Sorry, I forget that sometimes."

A moment later, the door to the penthouse opened, and Grey strode down the entrance hall into the living area. "Anything interesting happen while I was out?"

I hadn't been going to mention anything about Horus, but Eva, still across the room, piped up. "Mom got invited to a ball by an ass, but she's not going."

Grey turned to me with bemused confusion on his face. "I think that requires explaining."

He strode over and sat across from Ramsey and me, but before either of us could speak, he saw the invitation and picked it up.

"My cousin, Horus-the-dickhead, invited Ana to a ball," Ramsey said. "He hasn't met her, but he thinks he can steal her away from me."

"Not likely," Grey said, as he scanned the invitation.

"She's already decided, she's not going," Ramsey said.

Grey hummed for a moment. "Except..." He looked up at Ramsey who grunted and bristled.

"Except?" I asked.

"She said she's not going," Ramsey insisted before Grey could answer. Then he turned to me. "You're not going."

I sighed and looked at the huge man, feeling his rage swelling, a palpable heat rapidly growing at the edge of my senses. I probably should have been scared of him in a state like this, but I wasn't. I knew he'd never hurt me.

I raised a single brow in challenge. "You're going to tell your goddess what she can and cannot do?"

He opened his mouth, then snapped it shut, jaw tight. He'd learned his lesson, even if he didn't like it.

Good boy.

"I don't really want to go," I told him. "But I am curious why Grey thinks I should. I'm going to hear him out."

Ramsey's jaw twitched and chaos swirled in his eyes, but he didn't argue with me.

When I looked back to Grey, he was meeting Ramsey's fury with ease and smiling at me as if to say, *that's my goddess.*

"This ball will attract a lot of gods and daemons," Greys said. "It'll be a great place for you to scout for your parents. Also—" this was to Ramsey, "—if you, Fen, and I go as her escorts, I highly doubt Horus would try anything."

Ramsey huffed but didn't argue.

I nodded. "If I skip this, will there be other opportunities to meet the various gods and daemons?"

"Probably," Grey said with a shrug. "But every event

will draw a slightly different crowd. Your best shot to meet everyone will be to attend as many as you can."

That made sense. Also, I did like the idea of my three brawny men being my sexy escorts.

"I think that's reasonable." I turned to Ramsey. "What do you think?"

His midnight-blue gaze met mine, all power and fury for a moment before that faded and he drew in a deep breath.

"Yeah, you're right. I don't know why I was worried. You're powerful enough to resist Horus, and with the rest of us there, he won't try anything." He flashed me a devilish grin. "And the thought of showing you off to everyone, including Horus, now *that* appeals to me."

His gaze grew heated, which got me all hot and bothered, and as petty as it was, a part of me really liked the idea of being arm candy and "shown off" to the other gods.

"Done," I said.

Eva crawled up to lean on the back of the couch across the room.

"So does this mean a shopping trip to pick up a new dress for the party?" She beamed.

Eva and I — sharing the aspect of sex — both *loved* to go shopping to find new and sexy things to wear. We'd rarely gone together though, since we'd been at each other's throats most of our lives. The thought of a mother-daughter shopping trip with her was very appealing. That said, I had a different idea.

"I'd love that," I said to her. "But perhaps another time. I think I already have the perfect dress."

When I'd gone shopping for dresses — and spent way too much — in preparation for my job at Elysium, I'd bought one dress I wasn't sure I'd ever wear at the bar, as it had been far too fancy. But I'd been unable to resist it, since it looked simply stunning on me.

"Wanna see it?" I asked Eva.

"Absolutely!" she said with glee.

By the time we'd made it to my room, Reia and Caia had joined us. They waited in the main bedroom, Ramsey and Grey standing guard by the door, while Eva helped me get changed in the bathroom. Once Eva had helped me into the dress, we both stared at it for a long moment in a full-length mirror.

"Oh, wow..." Eva breathed.

"Yeah, I know," I said, hushed and reverent.

What made the dress so stunning was how it emphasized all my glorious features.

Blue and silver embroidered lace, sheer and delicate, covered two black silk panels down my front. The panels met at the low-slung waist, creating a deep-plunging V-shape. This displayed my ample cleavage — and a fair bit of side boob — as my full breasts strained against the material.

A single delicate clasp connected the two front panels behind my neck, leaving my back fully uncovered.

The silk brocade waist — the same black covered with silver and blue embroidery — clung tight to the top of my hips at the sides, but plunged lower in the back, showing off the top of my ass.

The skirt had two layers. Soft, black silk, fell to my ankles with high slits up the front of both legs. Over that was a sheer dress of black lace with silver and blue embroidery in delicate patterns, showing everything off while covering it elegantly at the same time.

I did a twirl and the dress flared out a little.

"You'll definitely turn heads in this," Eva said. "Can I borrow it when you're done?"

"Sure," I said. "Just don't ruin it."

"Would I do that?" she asked with mock innocence which made us both laugh.

When I strutted out — doing my best runway model impression — Reia and Caia gasped, eyes going wide, while Ramsey didn't move a muscle. Hunger burned in his midnight blue eyes, and a rather substantial bulge grew in his pants. Grey's smile was soft and warm, but his eyes glittered as if seeing the treasure at the end of some long quest.

"Wow," Grey breathed.

I did another twirl. "How do I look?"

Ramsey's tone was low and heated, a guttural growl of desire. "You're fucking gorgeous, Silverlocks. I don't know how I'm going to keep myself from slamming you against a wall and having my way with you."

"Annnnnd, that's our cue to leave." Eva laughed as she ushered Reia and Caia out.

Once they were gone, my two guys came to me, Ramsey pressing to me in front with Grey hot behind me.

"What were you saying about having your way with me?" I breathed as Ramsey's cock strained and throbbed against my stomach. Something about my aspect of sex just loved to drive men mad with longing.

"You need to get out of that dress now, Silverlocks, unless you want me to rip it off you."

I could almost hear the tearing of fabric, a sound that always sent bolts of lightning through my veins and super-heated my core. But there was no way I was going to let anyone ruin this dress. It was far too expensive.

Except before I could say that to Ramsey, he stepped back from me and Grey caught me from behind, clutching me close as Ramsey's feral gaze consumed me.

"Actually," Ramsey growled. "I have an even better idea."

Oh? I was desperate to hear it, and I squirmed, all hot and bothered against Grey. "Yeah?"

"Oh, yeah." He looked past me, over my shoulder to Grey. "She's all yours tonight. As long as she can be all mine tomorrow before the ball. I'll bring a limo around at seven-thirty. You and Fen can find your own way there. I have plans for Ana, in that dress, in the limo."

Oh...? Too bad I'd have to wait until then. But... that's when it hit me. The anticipation in Ramsey's eyes was suddenly matched in my heart. It would be the wait that would drive us both crazy...

"As long as you don't ruin the dress on the way to the party," I said.

Ramsey chuckled. "No, I won't ruin the dress at all. I'll just ruin *you*."

His growl of desire and the simmering need in his eyes was almost too much. I clamped my legs together to stop the flood of wetness threatening to gush out of me, and he saw my aroused distress and chuckled.

"Until then, Silverlocks," he whispered, then left.

Gods, I was so fucking horny. I spun in Grey's arms. "You need to get this dress off me and get your cock in me."

"How can I resist an offer like that?" he breathed. And the dress was off — and hung neatly — in record time. Which left me naked and Grey still fully dressed.

I couldn't wait for him to undress. Pulling his head down to mine I crashed our lips together, thrusting my tongue into his mouth as his hands roamed my heated flesh.

"Do you care if I ruin your suit?" I gasped, clinging to him, suddenly desperate with need.

He chuckled. "Not at all, go ahead."

I knew his suits were uber-expensive, hand-tailored, and exquisite, but right now... I didn't care.

I undid his belt, then slipped my hands into the waistband of his pants and used all my aspect-of-war strength to tear them open. They split easily, along with his boxers, freeing his cock.

I pushed him back and he stepped out of his ruined

pants. Another couple of steps and I pushed him down to sit on the edge of the bed. I straddled him, dropping my achingly wet and ready pussy onto his long shaft with a cry and a mini-orgasm as he filled me.

With a growl, I grabbed his shirt and ripped it off him. Buttons popped, fabric tore, and I came in a fucking flood as the sound slashed through me. Grey's hands on my hips pinned me down to his lap as I shuddered and writhed through my orgasm.

And once I'd thoroughly soaked his lap with my release without him having so much as done a single thrust, he chuckled. "Satisfied?"

"Oh, yeah," I purred between gasping breaths.

"Good. Now it's my turn."

Except he didn't move for a moment, and I shivered with anticipation at what he had in mind.

The trouble was... I really had no clue.

Ramsey I could trust to be primal and hard, a mountain of desire crashing down on me. Fen had sweet words and his super tongue and was always so patient and giving. But Grey could be anything, sometimes patient and giving, sometimes commanding and powerful, sometimes hard and needful. Curious, I tapped into my sex aspect to feel Grey's desires.

I felt his welling passion, his yearning for me, the sexual heat pulsing through him. But it was all just a little too contained. Everything Grey did was orderly and organized and his emotions were all kept in their own boxes, even his desire.

Well, screw that. I didn't know what he had in mind, but suddenly I knew what I wanted.

"I want you to lose control with me," I whispered to him. "Let go of your need to control everything and just fuck me with all your passion blazing forth. Can you do that, my love?"

Hesitation filled his eyes, even as his mouth quirked in a lopsided grin.

"I'm not sure I've ever fully lost control before," he breathed. "With my void, I... I've always been afraid of what it would do if I didn't rein it in."

"Maybe it's time you found out. Maybe fully unleashing it is what will help you finally take control of it." I wasn't sure of the logic there, but it seemed possible. "Don't think, just act. Take me, Grey. Unleash all your pent-up emotions. I want all of you."

I kissed him, a long and deep merging of passion, and when I drew back, just enough that my lips brushed over his, I whispered, "I can use my sex to help you feel all your passion. Do you want that? I do."

He was trembling as my hands slid over his shoulders and arms. "What if I hurt you?"

"I'll heal," I told him.

"What if... I can't regain control?" he whispered, his voice so soft I barely heard him, and something told me I'd just cut to this powerful man's deepest fear.

"Do you love me?"

"Yes, always."

"Trust in our love."

I didn't know how that would help, but some part of me knew that was what would sustain us through what was to come. I didn't know why, but I just knew we had to do this. Somehow my sexual need for Grey to lose control had turned into some sort of growth experience for him.

"Will you do this for me, my love?" I asked. "Will you do this... for you?" Then, just to cut the still seriousness which had built up around us. I wiggled my hips over him, squirming on his cock. "Please," I begged.

A single shudder pulsed through his body and his void swirled, completely filling his eyes.

"For you, Ana, I'll do anything."

Then he unleashed himself on me.

GREY

I trusted Ana implicitly. I loved her and knew her power, so I had to hope that some aspect of hers would be able to rein me in once I'd fully lost myself.

I'd never attempted anything like this before. Even when fighting Nari and taking my void to the brink of its limits, I'd still held a shred of control.

This would be a complete and utter surrender. I'd let loose and pour everything I was into Ana, all the good and the bad.

The sexiest woman in existence, naked on my lap, with my cock buried deep inside her, smiled softly and kissed me gently.

"Thank you," she whispered.

And I dropped all my restraints.

Her sex aspect had already surged my passion and desire, but now everything else that I was billowed forth as well. The centuries of pent-up anger at my father, the adoration for all the animals I'd saved and helped, all my achievements, all my failures. All that I was... I gave to her.

Gripping her, I rose from the bed, spun, and pushed her down onto the mattress, all while keeping my cock sheathed inside her. I spread her legs open so I could see her gleaming, wet folds, then gripped my hands over the tops of her thighs as I savagely pounded all my myriad emotions into her.

It was hard and vicious sex, but Ana didn't seem to mind. She threw her arms out to the sides, hands fisting the sheets, head pressed back, silver eyes rolling up, and mouth open in a silent scream. Her back arched, thrusting her breasts up, and I couldn't help myself, I shifted my hands from her thighs to those glorious orbs and squeezed, using them as my new anchor point as I drove myself relentlessly into her.

My vision blurred as my void finally and fully released. It sought to suck in and destroy everything around me...

Except it didn't.

There was only a split second, a fraction of a moment, where my void was completely unleashed, and I felt the world begin to collapse into me.

And then I stopped it.

Even if Ana was a goddess and powerful, she'd be consumed too. I'd known it in that instant, and I couldn't allow it. As she'd said, my love for her, our love, had guided me, stopped me. And in that same instant, I finally gained full control of my void.

It happened so fast I almost couldn't register it with everything else going on. Just like that — in a moment of full surrender — I'd gained the control I'd spent my entire life fighting for.

I'd spent so long holding myself back, terrified of ever fully letting loose, and miraculously, she'd discovered the one way for me to dominate my void.

Letting go with trust and love.

And with that, the tidal wave of all my other emotions flooding out of me was amplified with love and desire for this amazing woman.

I slammed my cock into her, then stopped.

"Yes," she cried out. "Come, my love!"

But that wasn't why I'd stopped.

"I love you, Ana!" The words were torn from me as a scream of ragged joy mixed with all my other jumbled emotions.

I loved her because she'd just shown me one very simple truth which had eluded me all of my very long life: you could never hope to control yourself until you'd fully allowed yourself to lose control.

All my emotions were still tumbling through me, but now that I'd allowed them out, I knew I could live with them, could understand and govern them.

I would have never reached this point of utter awareness if it hadn't been for Ana, and I knew then, she deserved far more than just some rough sex from me.

I pulled my cock out, drenched in her wetness, and knelt to plant my face between her thighs. I licked her juices from her legs, then clamped my mouth over her pussy and used just a touch of my void to create the most amazing suction on her.

"Oh, great fucking gods!" she cried out, and her body shook with a powerful orgasm. She flooded my mouth and my void sucked the wave of her wetness down, seeking more, more more more.

Leaving her blessed entrance, I pushed myself up her body, kissing with void-infused lips, leaving red marks on her stomach where I'd sucked her flesh. Then I sealed my lips over one nipple, flicking my tongue over the tight bud as I sucked her deep into my mouth.

"Fuck me!" she whimpered, but I wasn't ready to resume with my cock just yet so I pushed two fingers into her, found her g-spot, and thrust into that as my thumb swirled around her clit.

And when I popped off her nipple, the flesh all puffy and red and swollen, she came again, inspiring me to do the same with her other breast.

"Grey, yes, whatever this is, it's amazing!" Ana shouted through her bliss.

I pulled back and stood over her, taking in her deliciously sinful form: sweaty and flushed, disheveled and pleasured. Her legs were pressed back, open wide, her hips thrusting up, even though there was nothing for her glistening pussy to push against.

I used my hand — drenched in her wetness — to stroke my cock, coating it again, then slapped my length down on her clit several times, which caused her to cry out and squirm even more. I wanted her pleasure to go on forever, even as my own tornado of unrelenting bliss — along with every other feeling I had — swirled inside me.

"Please," she whimpered.

I knew what she was asking for, my release, for me to lose control inside her.

"Yes, my goddess," I whispered, slapping my cock down one last time on her clit before slipping down her folds and thrusting deep inside her.

Her legs wrapped around me, clamping tight, keeping me close. I gripped her sides and pulled her up from the bed. I wanted her next to me while I plunged with abandon into her well-pleasured pussy.

She wrapped her arms around my neck and merged her lips with mine in a ferocious kiss. Her hips rocked and bounced, and I added a touch of my void again, sucking the breath from her, even as I poured forth all my unrestrained desire into her with savage thrusts.

I didn't have to hold her up, since her legs had a death-grip on my waist, so I slid my hands up to the still-swollen tips of her breasts and teased those extremely sensitive nubs.

Her pussy clamped around my cock, pulsating and milking me, even as she flooded once again. She gasped the last of her breath into my mouth, her eyes rolling up again, and I released her to get some air, as I void-sucked her bottom lip until it was swollen and plump.

Fuck Grey, please! she screamed into my soul. *I can't believe how amazing you are! I need to feel you come... but don't be surprised if I pass out from pleasure when you do.*

Then touch me with your sex, make me explode, I whispered into her soul.

Yes! she cried out.

Her sex aspect filled my cock, swollen and super-sensitive, ready to release.

Yes! Now!

But I teased both of us by using my void to stop me from coming.

Ana surged her sex more and more, dragging me — with painful intensity — toward my release.

Pleeeeeaaaase! she screamed inside me, and I couldn't take it any longer.

I released my void and roared.

It felt like I truly exploded inside her. Radiant bliss overwhelmed me for a moment, and I staggered, falling with Ana onto the bed as we both reached some new height of ecstasy.

She did pass out, even as her body kept clutching and writhing and shuddering, while I couldn't stop coming. My balls grew tight, but then Ana's sex seemed to refresh them and squeeze them dry again and again.

I was still roaring with my utterly savage pleasure as Ana returned to herself and cried out yet again. Her arms wrapped around me, holding me close, as we both pulsed with our seemingly unending releases. I kissed her lips, and she gasped, her bottom lip still swollen and sensitive.

"What... was that?" Ana asked once she'd regained her breath, her body still quivering with aftershocks of bliss.

"My void. I... I learned to control it," I said with a breathy laugh. "When I unleashed it fully, it was going to tear you apart and I couldn't let that happen, so... I stopped it. That was the key. I had to release it to control it."

She gave a soft chuckle. "Sort of like, if you love something set it free and it will come back."

"Sort of."

"I'm glad." Then she shivered. "Those void kisses... just... wow. My nipples have never felt so sensitive and... you literally took my breath away. That was... a bit of a high, though not one I think I want to repeat." She shuddered again. "You're still coming," she breathed in awe.

"You're still a ravishingly alluring sex goddess. Can you blame me?"

Another chuckle. "Nope, I guess not. But I think we're making quite the mess on your bed."

"Just this side. The other side will be fine to sleep on tonight, and I'll get another one tomorrow." I was going through beds at a rather astonishing rate, but it was so worth it. I kissed her bottom lip again, carefully breathing hot air on it before brushing my lips over it, making Ana whine and shiver.

"Thank you," I whispered to her. "You were right. I

needed to lose control. I feel... whole now, in a way I never have before."

"Sexual healing, that's what I'm here for," she whispered, her breath catching as her bottom lip brushed past mine. "I'm so primed and sensitive right now, I could probably come on command."

"Oh?" I said with a curious grin and I lowered my face next to hers — shifting on top of her at the same time for a bit of added stimulation — and flicked my tongue over the shell of her ear, whispering, "Come for me, beautiful."

And she did.

Much later, when we'd both finally come down, we showered, then had dinner with her kids. Eva kept winking at me, while Reia and Caia couldn't meet my eyes.

I was going to have to soundproof my room.

That night — after a thoroughly exhausted Ana had fallen asleep with her head resting on my chest — I lay awake for a while, reveling in the peace and stillness within my soul. My void was gone. I'd banished it, but I knew I could draw it back when needed. And that, along with all of the emotional baggage I'd released that afternoon, made me feel far more relaxed and serene than I ever had.

FEN

THE ELYSIUM CLUB SHOULD HAVE BEEN BUSY WITH A DINNER rush, but it was close to empty. Most of the daemons who would usually be here were probably getting ready for Horus' party tonight which made it the perfect place for a quiet conversation among friends.

Since Ramsey had begged to be the one to take Ana to the ball, that left Grey and me at loose ends. We'd meet them there, but for now... we could have a little chat.

A chat that might require alcohol.

"Thanks, Maria," I said to the small human bartender.

"Any time, Wolfy," she said, setting down the bottle of Helfyr Whiskey and bringing out two shot glasses. "Something on your mind?" she inquired, as all good bartenders do.

"Yes, but it's for me to discuss with someone else." I

picked up the bottle and two glasses, and Maria shrugged and moved away.

I sauntered across the lounge to where Grey sat, already decked out in a perfectly tailored black suit, and set my things down on the table and sat opposite him. I, too, was all preened and pretty, in a navy shirt and a silver-blue suit, to match Ana's eyes.

Grey was unusually calm and relaxed today, no void swirling in his sable-black eyes.

"You're different," I commented, curious if he'd elaborate.

"I am." He grinned. "Ana changed me. She got me to master my void and deal with five thousand years of emotional baggage, all with one perfect session of sex."

I grinned. "Yeah, she can do that." Not that I'd experienced what he'd just described, but I'd learned that our amazing Ana could do pretty much anything she put her mind to. "I'm glad."

He smiled, which was also uncharacteristic for him. "So, you wanted to chat?"

I poured out two full shot glasses of the whisky and handed him one.

"I want to talk about that last time we were all together with Ana," I began. "Specifically, I want to talk about... our kiss."

"Ah," Grey said. Then he picked up the shot glass and downed the contents in one go.

I did the same with mine, even though I didn't really need it. The kiss had been no big deal for me, in fact, I'd enjoyed it. And really, who in their right mind, wouldn't? Grey was gorgeous and a great kisser.

"What about it?" he said, a little gruff and distant.

Ah. So it was going to be like that.

"I liked it," I said softly. I didn't want to push too hard, but I didn't want him denying himself, either. "And I'm fairly certain, you did too."

"It pleased Ana," he said, his gaze wandering to the far side of the bar even as his lips curled into a half smile. "That's what *I* liked about it."

"I'm pretty sure it was more than that," I pushed. "I was the one in your mouth at the time, and my tongue is pretty sensitive."

"What does Ana call it?" he asked with a chuckle. "Your miracle tongue?"

"Yeah, exactly." But he was getting a little off topic. My tongue wasn't the issue. I leaned forward. "Come on, man. It's the twenty-first century, and you're a *Greek daemon*, for Asgard's sake! Your culture practically *invented* male-male love. Why is this so hard for you? You can't tell me you're still harboring some silly notion that being with a man makes you less of a man somehow."

He sighed, looking away for a moment. "Maybe... I'm just... confused."

"Confused because you love Ana," I guessed, "and it felt good kissing me, which somehow feels like you're betraying her?"

"Yeah, something like that."

"Ah..."

That would explain his hesitancy. He wasn't being weird about it because he wasn't into it, but because he was in love with Ana.

I poured us both another shot.

"And the fact that it was Ana telling us to do it, and she really got off on it... that doesn't tell you something?" I asked.

He turned back, his dark eyes studying me for a moment. "You think she wants us to be together?"

I picked up my glass and waited. He picked up his, and we did another shot.

The Helfyr burned all the way down and I let out a satisfied, "Ahhhh," and sighed.

"Yes, I do." But I could feel in my soul that Ana wanted more than just to see us hook up. She was a goddess of love after all. "Let me ask you this, Grey. Do you think there will ever be anyone for you other than Ana?"

"No." He answered quickly without a second thought.

"Exactly. It's the same for me. We're both one-woman men now. But what that means is that both of us, and Ramsey, are essentially married to Ana. We're all in this together. So... why not enjoy each other's company." I poured two more glasses and raised mine.

He took his and reluctantly clinked it against mine and we both drank.

"I don't think Ramsey would be into any of this, but you," I said. "I think you might be, and I figured we should get it out into the open if you are." I gave a soft laugh. "It'll make cuddling in bed afterward a lot easier if we don't mind holding each other as well. So... what do you say?"

He grunted. "I suppose I shouldn't be surprised that Loki's son is bi."

"More... pan than bi."

"Ah... yeah, right." Grey laughed, poured himself another shot, and slung it back. He thought for a moment, then said, "Here's the thing. I don't think I'd want to be with you outside of being with Ana."

"That's fair. But," I said, testing the waters, "if she asked us to put on a show for her, get each other worked up, would you go for that?"

He nodded. "Yeah, I would."

"And who knows," I added, "perhaps in a thousand years, you won't mind being with me separately."

"Anything's possible," he replied. "Is that what *you* want?"

I laughed. "Honestly, I don't know. I know kissing you to turn Ana on was surprisingly sexy. As for being with you without Ana... well... it never hurts to keep your options open. As long as Ana's okay with it, and I think she would be, then who knows?"

Grey nodded. Then his brow furrowed, his gaze distant for a long moment.

I took a guess at his thoughts. "You're thinking about kissing Ramsey, aren't you?"

He looked up at me. "Can't quite picture it. How about you?"

"He's a sexy guy... again... who knows?" I shrugged.

"You're far more accepting than—"

"Oh, Zaggy! There you are! Give your big sisters a hug!"

A wild woman came flying — literally flying — across the lounge and tackled Grey. The two of them crashed to the ground, destroying the chair he'd been sitting on.

Since I'd already met two of his sisters, I assumed this was the third: Erini. Though, from what I'd heard of her, she was actually three sisters in one.

Erini was all three of the Ancient Greek Furies, all rolled into a single, wild package. She could separate and become the three sisters: Tisiphone, Alecto, and Megara, but she rarely did. Each of those three was only a minor daemon, but together she was on the level of a minor god.

She had the same Mediterranean-tanned skin as her brother, with similar — though much longer — thick black hair. She wasn't tall, but she was built sturdily with heavy hips and thighs and strong arms, a body meant for tackling younger brothers. I should know, my older sister Hel was of a similar build.

"Get off me, Erini!" Grey said from somewhere below her, groaning a little.

She popped up from where she sat on Grey and looked at me.

"Hey there!" she said, excited. "You're Fenris, aren't you!"

"In the flesh," I said with a flourish of my hand. "And you're Erini, yes?"

Her dark-brown eyes, ringed with hell-fire-red, went wide. "You've heard of me? Oh, wow! I knew it."

"Knew that I'd heard of you?"

"Knew we were meant for each other!" she said jumping up and throwing herself at me. I reacted just a bit too slowly and found her latched onto me like a giant leech.

"Erini! Get off him!" Grey shouted as he rose. "He doesn't want you."

"But we're both daemons of destruction!" she said cheerily, rubbing her bosom — which had nothing on Ana's — over me as her hand slid into my pants.

"Whoa!" I reacted viscerally, my wolf coming out for just a second to lend some strength as I leaped up and tossed her off me.

"Is this how you want me? On my knees?" she asked looking up at me from the floor. Before I could answer she looked over at Grey. "Why didn't you tell me you were friends with Fenris?"

"Didn't think it mattered," Grey said, dusting himself off.

"Of course it does, Zaggy. You know I've been searching for a soulmate, one who likes to destroy things as much as I do." She looked back at me, that hellfire in her eyes now literally blazing and burning. "And now I've found him!"

She was crazy. That was clear.

"I've already got a soulmate, thanks," I said.

"Fen, no!" Grey had tried to say while I'd been talking, and I found out why a second later.

"Then I'll just kill her and have you all to myself," Erini said with a manic grin. "I'll show you how much we're meant to be together, my love! I'll show you!" That sounded too much like a threat.

I needed to get away from this madwoman, but also didn't want to leave her with Grey.

"Ah..." I said, not knowing what to say.

"There you are!" Came an all too familiar, booming voice. It was the last person I wanted to see... usually. But right now...

"Sorry, Erini, I've got to run, my father's calling me. And we wouldn't want to piss off Loki, now would we?" I turned to Grey and mouthed the word "sorry," then bolted.

Loki had just entered the lounge, and I got to him before he'd taken another step.

My father was devilishly handsome — or beautiful — in whatever form he decided to take, but his natural form was truly striking. Thick waves of golden-blond hair cascaded around his face and over his shoulders. Fair-featured, his face was narrow and all sharp edges, with pale-blue eyes like ice, and a mouth tilted in a knowing smirk. He was slender and tall, but far stronger than he looked. The two of us had never really gotten along because he loved that I was a world-ending daemon... and I didn't.

He brushed some of those luscious locks back from his shoulder.

"That's a good boy. You're such a good boy aren't you!"

He also loved treating me like a puppy.

A suspicious look sparked in his eyes. "But you usually don't come when I call, so... what's up, little wolf?"

"Nothing," I said.

I'd learned over the centuries that to Loki, information was power and I shouldn't tell him anything. He still had ways of finding things out, but I'd never give him the satisfaction of making it easy. He'd have to work for it.

"What do you want, father?" I asked, my tone gruff. He may have saved me from dealing with Erini, but I still didn't much like talking to him.

"Always so formal, Fenny." Loki laughed, then shook his head. "What happened to my little puppy that liked to tear up Asgard and destroy everything?"

"I grew up."

Loki frowned. That was never a good sign. Loki never got mad, he got mischievous, and that was always bad.

Then he huffed. "You're such a disappointment. I expected so much more from my little world-ender. I know you can't officially destroy everything until Ragnarök, but you could at least be causing *some* havoc. But noooo... you insist on working human jobs. That's so very beneath your potential, my son."

Son?

Something was up. He never called me son.

"I like what I do. I'm happy," I told him.

"You shouldn't be happy. You should be ravenously tearing up the world." He shook his head and his ice-cold eyes bored into me. "And what's this I hear about you falling for some pretty young goddess?"

Fuck. He knew about Ana.

That was very bad. I hadn't expected to keep her a secret forever, but still...

"Stay away from her, or I swear I'll—"

"She's a goddess, I wouldn't dream of touching her," he said, his high-pitched laugh cut me off as his frozen eyes twinkled. "Though, I wonder if she'd notice if I visited her looking like you? Is she as sweet as they say? I might like to taste her." He laughed again as I fumed. "But no, I'm not here to play with your little goddess. No, I'm here to play with *you*, my puppy."

Oh, fuck, that was definitely not good. Loki's "playing" had caused The Black Plague and the Bermuda Triangle.

I backed away, though I knew I'd never escape him. He was supernaturally fast, blinking from place to place with ease.

Suddenly that piercing laugh of his was freezing my very bones.

"I think it's time you remembered your roots, little puppy," my father said with a wide grin. "Time to take your wolf for a walk. *Consume! Destroy!*" There was power infused into those last words, which thrummed through me.

"No!" I gasped.

Except even as I turned to run, Loki was there on the other side of me, having moved faster than I could see. He reached out one gracefully long finger, touching my forehead, and I was instantly unable to move. That touch held me, boring into my mind, suppressing me while calling my wolf.

No!

The word died on my lips, unspoken. I was no longer in control. That was the power of Loki. One touch and I was helpless before him. He'd easily pushed me down into my own subconscious and summoned my beast, ready to explode forth with ravenous fury.

Yet... I only partially shifted. My wolf didn't fully emerge, and confused dismay clouded my father's expression.

"What...?"

I was just as shocked as he was. Except before he could tear apart my mind to find out how I had resisted him, my beast tore itself away from him. He may have been able to overpower me, but my beast far exceeded even Loki's abilities.

And with the sliver of control I still had, I ran, bolting for an elevator — just as one opened and an unsuspecting daemon walked out. I slammed myself inside, my pulse pounding, relieved to see the door close on Loki's still confused face.

When the elevator door opened, I staggered away, out of the lobby. People ran and screamed when they saw me.

My wolf was straining to be fully free and take control, but it couldn't. Still, I was half shifted, my hybrid form terrifying to any normal person.

I stumbled through the streets of Manhattan, trying to regain control, but I couldn't. Throwing myself into an alley, I raked my claws across my chest. The pain helped to clear my mind for a moment, so I could hopefully figure out what was happening.

Why hadn't I fully shifted? How had I been able to resist my father?

If I could figure that out, perhaps I'd be able to regain full control.

I saw Ana's divine face in my mind, and she reached out and ran a hand through my hair.

I love you, Fen, she whispered, *you can do this!*

It wasn't actually her, just a vision, but still... it gave me the enlightenment I needed. My soul, including my beast, belonged to Ana now. Her love sustained me, strengthened me, to the point that I'd been able to resist my father's compulsion.

Except Loki had still called Fenris forth and without more help from Ana, my wolf would emerge soon.

And while my beast may love Ana as much as I did, it also still loved to destroy and consume and it was straining to do just that.

I pushed myself out of the alley, staggering and stumbling like a drunkard. Luckily, people got out of my way, because I still looked like a fucking werewolf. I couldn't help that. It took everything I had to simply put one foot in front of the other.

I had to get to Horus' party. I knew I'd find Ana there.

Because if I didn't find her, a lot of people were going to die tonight.

GREY

Erini was drooling over Fen, her wild eyes fixated on the man as he fled to his father, then she used a finger to wipe up her saliva, sticking it in her mouth and licking it off.

"Tell me everything about him, Zaggy!" she exclaimed. "I must know how to capture my man. And who is this woman he's seeing? Tell me where she is so I can kill her... slowly." Her smile was manic. She wasn't kidding and was actually excited about ending another goddess, even if doing so would have nasty repercussions for her.

"Fuck off, Erini," I hissed.

Those gleeful, wild eyes turned dark. Her head tilted too far to one side. "You won't deny me, *brother*." Except her smile didn't fade. "You remember that time I took you to Tartarus to play?"

I did. I'd been young and she'd been deceptively nice

for once. I'd been itching to get out of father's palace in the underworld, so, she'd taken me to Tartarus, the lowest of the realms of Hades, where the worst of the worst were tormented.

She'd tortured me there for months before father had realized I was missing and gone looking for me. I was a daemon, and killing me wasn't easy, but I still felt pain and she'd known exactly how to cause the most agony while making sure I stayed alive and mostly well. She'd laughed the entire time, and when father had found me, he hadn't even punished her. He'd told me to be more careful, that pain was just in Erini's nature.

I'd left Hades not long after that.

"I'm stronger now," I said to Erini. "You won't find me as easy to deceive or capture."

Yet she was still a minor goddess and even with my void fully under control, she was probably stronger than I was.

And she proved it the next moment, flashing in — faster than I could evade — to grasp my throat with a clawed hand.

"You'll tell me what I want to know, Zaggy." She dug her nails into my neck. "Or I'll rip out your throat." Her eyes twinkled. Then her grin grew. "No. I'll tear out your heart, take from you what you love most. I'll go attack your little animal shelters. I'll tear all those innocent animals to shreds. How would you like that?"

Fuck, she knew me too well.

Except I grinned in the face of her — frighteningly lucid — insanity.

"I'm the Lord of Conquest, sister. If you do that. I swear I'll hunt you to the ends of the earth and trap you in some dark spot where all your power amounts to nothing."

It wasn't an idle threat. With enough planning, my aspect of The Hunt could take down those a lot stronger than me.

"You remember when Cousin Hercules challenged me to capture him?" I said. "I was able to seal that big oaf away where even his strength couldn't help him. He'd never have gotten out, if he hadn't admitted I'd won and asked me to release him. I'll do the same to you, sister. If you touch my shelters or Fen or his woman, I swear, I'll make you pay."

I surged my void then, staring Erini down.

She flinched back as my void began to tear at her. She possessed the aspect of destruction and could counter my void... to a point, but...

"Ugh! I always hated your void!" She released me and backed away. I reined in my void. "What do you care about Fen's hussy?" Her dark eyes narrowed slightly before widening with realization.

Fuck.

"You love her too, don't you? The filthy slut has captured the heart of my little brother and my true love. She must die!" And with that Erini vanished from where she stood.

"Fuck me," I whispered, as I massaged my bleeding throat.

It was only a matter of time before Erini found Ana. It wouldn't be too hard. Ana *was* living with me at the moment.

That said, Ana was a goddess herself and possessed the aspect of war. Also, her many aspects would make her inherently more powerful than Erini. Still, Erini possessed the aspects of destruction, rage, and envy, and all to their fullest extremes. She was also much older and more experienced in her power than Ana. I didn't know who would win in a fight between them, and I didn't want to find out.

I pulled out my phone and called Ana.

She picked up quickly.

"Hey there, sexy," she purred on the other end of the line.

"Ana, I'm afraid we have a situation with another of my sisters."

She sighed. "Another one? Again?"

"Yes, and this one's far more powerful than Melinoe. Her name is Erini, and she's a minor goddess with aspects of destruction, rage, and envy. And right now, you're the target of her jealousy and she wants to rage-kill you. Sorry."

"Whatever," Ana said, non-plussed. "Let her come. I'm a warrior now, I can defend myself."

I smiled. "Yeah, you can, but I still wanted to give you a heads up."

"Thanks, Grey," she said softly. Then, "I'm sorry your family is so messed up."

"Yeah, me too."

"Ramsey will be here shortly to take me to the ball," she said. "Should I still go?"

"You'll be surrounded by other daemons and gods," I told her. "Erini would have to be truly crazy to go after you there."

"What about my daughters? Would she come after them?"

Would she? I didn't think so, but then... she *had* just threatened my shelters as a way to get to me. "She's not usually that indirect in her thinking, but it's possible. If they stay together, with Kerberos to guard them, they should be safe. If you want, I can skip the party and keep an eye on them."

"You'd do that? For me?" she asked.

"Any day."

"You're amazing, thank you, Grey. I love you."

"Love you," I breathed.

We hung up, and I hurried out of Elysium and across town.

ANAIS

After Ramsey arrived, I'd explained about Grey's sister, and he'd immediately made a few calls.

Even with Grey at the apartment, Ramsey was concerned for my daughters — bless him — and wanted a bit more support. So, he'd called in a favor with his cousin, Anubis.

When Anubis arrived, he had the strangest beast with him. It had the head of a crocodile, with the mane and front end of a lion, then the back end of a hippo. Its name was Ammit, and it was certainly intimidating to look at.

"Should I ask?" I whispered to Ramsey.

He chuckled. "Ammit eats the hearts of evil-doers, but she's actually really cuddly if you get to know her."

Well, as guard animals went, that sounded like exactly what I'd want.

"Works for me," I said with a shrug.

Between Kerberos and Ammit, with Grey's void, Eva's

war, and Caia's healing... I figured my daughters would be okay if Grey's sister decided to visit.

Ramsey and I delayed leaving until Grey arrived. The tall daemon rushed in, looking a bit disheveled, and he gave me a quick kiss and told me not to worry. With him guarding my kids, I didn't.

"Stay close to her, tonight, just in case," Grey said to Ramsey.

Ramsey grunted with a smirk. "Of course."

Then, Ramsey and I went down to Grey's Bentley Mulsanne Grand Limousine, but the car didn't move once we were inside.

I looked questioningly at Ramsey.

"I asked the chauffeur for a little time before we left," he said, voice husky. "We ate up some of that waiting for Grey, but there should still be time for a little *fun*. Something to take your mind off... everything."

"Oh?" I asked, suddenly interested, tingling heat filtering through my body despite the revealing — and chilly — dress. "And... how exactly do you plan to distract me?" I asked, although I had a pretty good guess.

"I want to make sure Horus, and every other daemon and god, knows you're taken once we arrive," Ramsey said, slipping off the seat beside me to kneel on the floor in front of me.

"You going to chain us together?" I teased, waggling my eyebrows at him.

"No," he said, slowly sliding my dress up my legs. "But I figure having my cologne on your thighs would do it."

He opened my legs and I slid forward on the seat, pushing my dress the rest of the way up and presenting my naked pussy to him.

He leaned down and kissed my sensitive inner thighs, then rubbed his neck over them, marking his territory. With every press of his lips or flick of his tongue, the tension that had been gripping me tightly upstairs after Grey's dire news slowly melted away.

And when his seeking lips finally pressed to my folds, I gasped with a soft release, all my anxiety fading away completely.

"Are you going to make me come and ruin this nice dress?" I asked. My voice was already shaking as he dove fully into his oral assault on me.

He pulled back. "I figure you won't make too much of a mess if I lick up every last drop." He smiled, then pressed back in to do just that.

Oh, hell yes!

"Gods, you're so fucking sweet," he moaned.

His tongue flicked over my clit. Each lick of my sensitive bud sent shocking thrills of wet heat through my entire body. I moaned and pressed my head back against the seat, digging my hands into the plush cushions and rocking my hips against his face.

Usually Ramsey was all about himself, pleasuring me but also seeking his own release. But this... this was all giving. His cock must have been ragingly hard, but he took his time to give me this, help me relax more and more.

I wanted to urge him on, let him know how he was doing. "Yes, Ramsey," I whispered. "Yes, thank you, oh yes!" I shifted my hands from the seat to his head, fisting his hair.

And just as I reached the brink... as if he knew I was so very close... Ramsey pulled away, back to licking my thighs.

"Please!" I keened, trying to push his head back in.

"You ready to come, gorgeous?" he rasped, voice a little ragged.

"Yes!" I begged, hips moving but lacking anything to grind against.

"Want me to drink all your sweet nectar, Silverlocks?"

"Yes! Please! Ramsey!"

Ramsey moved back in with a long, slow lick of his tongue, which jerked me to the brink after having eased off a bit with his absence. Then he planted his lips over me, sucking hard, tongue flicking my clit before slipping down and darting into me.

"Oh gods, yes!" I cried as I flooded his mouth with my release.

He moaned in masculine satisfaction, tongue lapping over my drenched folds to urge out every last drop, and with my body and soul completely sated, I went limp, buzzed with bliss.

Still, Ramsey stayed latched to my pussy, cleaning up the mess he'd caused, before slowly pulling away, as if reluctant to do so.

"The nectar of the gods," he breathed. "I can see why

Fen likes licking you so much." He took another long breath. "Wow."

"I think that's what I'm supposed to say," I gasped as I slowly put my dress back into place, covering myself. I tapped my sex aspect and sapped any lingering lust from my loins to make sure I wouldn't make a mess, but I kept the feeling of besotted serenity that now coursed through me. "I'm definitely ready to face the world now."

"As I'd hoped," Ramsey said. He wiped his face with a handkerchief, then sat beside me again. "If you ever need a *top-up* this evening, let me know."

"You'd do that, for me?" I asked. "Without getting anything for yourself?"

He laughed. "I can be generous." He leaned over to kiss me lightly, the lemony-sweet taste of my release still on his tongue. Then he whispered. "You've given me many incredible highs and I know you will again in the future. Tonight... is all for you."

I smiled and sighed. "Good to know."

He drew back a little so it was easier to meet my gaze, and his midnight blue eyes were intense and earnest when he whispered, "Anything for you."

My heart swelled and pounded just a little bit faster.

The car was moving by then, and it wasn't long before we arrived at our destination.

But Fen wasn't there to greet us.

And despite the wonderful, anxiety-reducing bliss Ramsey had induced on the way here, I began to worry.

Fen wasn't the type to bail... not without calling or something.

"He's probably just a little late, or we're a little early or something," Ramsey tried to soothe me. "Don't worry, Silverlocks. He'll be here."

Except Fen was *never* late, so I *was* worried, but I tried to quell my uneasiness as Ramsey and I made our way inside.

ANAIS

W<small>E ENTERED THE HOTEL, AND INSTANTLY</small> I <small>WAS SWEPT UP</small> in the grandeur of the venue and the event. The lobby was decked to the nines, the doormen and bellhops wore tuxedos, and women in sparkling sequined gowns were ushering guests from upstairs or outside into the main ballroom, which was massive and decorated to the hilt. But the splendor of the room was nothing compared to those who mingled within it.

The only true goddess I'd met so far was Freyja, and before me now were dozens of deities, all lavishly attired, looking amazing.

Most of the men, like Ramsey, wore suits or tuxedos, although a few were draped in old fashioned robes or togas, and several even wore armor.

The women displayed a panoply of styles. From barely-there dresses, far more scandalous than mine, to regular ball gowns of all styles and colors, to older styles of dresses, or robes and togas like some of the men.

As Ramsey escorted me into the ballroom, I gawked at the array of powerful Empyreans around me. Not just because of how stunning they were, but because I could *feel* most of them. My daemon sense pinged off many of those around me to various degrees signaling their levels of power.

And yet — even with all these other sights to see — Ramsey couldn't take his eyes off me. And there were many others who admired my passing, which made me blush like a schoolgirl.

"Well, look at you!"

The semi-familiar voice caught my attention and I turned to see Freyja striding up to me. Unsurprisingly, she'd chosen the barely-there style of dress. It was practically a negligee, barely long enough to cover her ass. Two narrow panels of pale pink covered her front and back with slender strings tied over her shoulders and at the hem to keep them from flying away, and her magnificent breasts were barely contained by the not-quite-see-through silk, which made it clear she wasn't wearing anything underneath.

And still, Ramsey's eyes slid off her and back to me easily.

"That's quite the dress," Freyja said. "You might turn as many heads as I will, perhaps more, just from being the novelty of a newcomer." She gazed at me for a long moment. "And you've come into more power since last we met. Your aura is... impressive." She almost sounded jealous.

A tall, dark-skinned man, chest bared, wearing only a simple wrap skirt from waist to knees, approached from behind Freyja and draped a well-muscled arm over her shoulders.

"Hey there, Freyja darling." His dark eyes drank her in like he'd spent a hundred days parched in the desert, then they turned to me and I got the same treatment. "Do you and your friend want to find a room and show me all your treasures?"

"Back off, Min," Ramsey snarled. "You can do what you wish with Freyja, but Ana is mine!"

The tall man — even taller than Ramsey, which was impressive, though he wasn't nearly as thick with muscle — gave a relaxed, disarming smile. "Don't worry, cousin. I was just asking. Women are allowed to say no." His smile widened. "Though... most don't." He turned back to Freyja. Her small frame, pale and blond against his tall and dark, were quite the contrast. "You up for some fun?"

"With you Min? Always!"

The two sauntered off and left the ballroom.

"He seems... nice?" I said, a bit confused. Were propositions like this going to happen all night?

"Min is Horus' brother, god of sex and fertility. At least he wasn't walking around with a raging hard-on, which isn't uncommon."

Something told me there were going to be lots of godly "quirks" I would have to get used to.

"And... people just wander off to have sex?" I asked.

Ramsey scoffed. "Given the number of Empyreans devoted to beauty or sex or love or fertility or whatever... yeah that happens a lot. There are private rooms off the ballroom where couples or groups can go to get their freak on."

"Charming."

Another tall dark-skinned man approached. This one bore some faint resemblance to Ramsey — his proportions were certainly similar, large and tall and made for brute force. He was dressed in a bespoke tuxedo, perfectly fitted to his powerful frame.

"Fuck," Ramsey swore softly. "This may be unpleasant."

"Who—?" was all I got out before the man reached us.

"Ramsey," the man said in a voice very similar to Ramsey's himself. His midnight-black eyes were hard, especially when they passed over me, and it was clear he didn't like me. "Aren't you supposed to be handling Horus?"

"Hello, Father." Ah... that explained a lot. "Horus hasn't come down yet, I'll be heading up shortly to make sure he gets down here safely, so he can make his grand entrance."

"See that you do." Those hard eyes turned to me. "You must be the new goddess, Anais."

"Yes, your most reverent excellency," I said, bowing

my head slightly to him. I'd brushed up on my godly titles in preparation for tonight.

He scoffed. "I can see how you bewitched my son. You do have your *charms*." That word held just a little too much creepy interest for my liking and I suppressed a shiver of disgust. "But as I told him, love and strife don't mix. My son can't love anyone. He's using you. And when fucking is no longer fun, he'll leave you. If he doesn't. I'll make sure he does."

What a total douchebag. I now understood Ramsey's warning about "unpleasantness."

I met the god's dark-eyed gaze and, before I spoke, I measured his godly power, searching out his aspects. He had one which seemed like my aspect of war, another like Ramsey's chaos, and one more.

He only had three?

From what I'd learned of gods, power was relative and based on several factors.

Age was often the most significant. The longer a daemon or god had been around, the longer they'd had to develop their abilities.

The number of aspects was another. The greater the number of aspects, the more inherently powerful a god was.

This god was probably far older than me, but I was no slouch. And I had seven aspects to his three, even if my aspects of beauty and law weren't well developed yet.

I'd guess we'd see which of us was stronger, since I

wasn't about to let him say such things about Ramsey and me.

So... "Fuck you, your royal shitiness," I said evenly. "You wouldn't know love if it sat on your face. Not that anyone would want to sit on your ugly mug, buster. And if you *ever* try to tell Ramsey or me what to do again, even once, I'll cut you into little pieces. I swear it on my aspect of law and justice." Those last words seemed to thrum through me and I felt a surge of power.

Ramsey's father's eyes went wide.

Ramsey choked on a laugh.

"You little—"

I brought out my sword. "Consider your next words carefully." My tone was lethal.

Everyone around us hushed instantly, all except for one whispered voice who said, "Holy me, she's fucking hot and powerful!"

I had to grin at that.

The tall man glared daggers at me, but I knew he'd felt it too. I'd made an oath on an aspect of law and that had bound both of us. If he did as I'd described, I would have to act against him.

"Do your duty," the man spat at Ramsey, then turned and stalked away.

I put my sword away and looked at Ramsey. He was beaming at me with wide-eyed wonder.

"I don't think anyone has ever talked to Set that way before. And... he didn't even try to beat you down, which would have been his usual reaction. I think he was actually scared of you! Gods, you're incredible, Ana." He crushed me in a tight embrace as those around us slowly went back to what they were doing.

"How powerful is he?" I asked, curious.

Ramsey gave another choking laugh. "He's one of the greater gods of Egypt!"

"Oh..."

"And you told him off like he was a petulant schoolboy who'd thrown a tantrum."

"Well... he had. And what's this about you needing to go look after Horus?"

Ramsey sighed. "I'm in charge of keeping my idiot cousin in line. I'll need to go and tend to him at some point. But I'm sure we can find someone for you to chat with while I'm gone."

But that only reminded me that Fen hadn't arrived yet. I quickly pulled my phone from my small clutch and checked my messages.

Nothing.

Where was he?

I tried to hide my worry as Ramsey led me around the room and through a series of introductions that did a good job of keeping me occupied for a while, since most of these people were incredibly fascinating.

The more gods and daemons I met, the more I realized I should have been doing research about all of them. I didn't know how they could keep track of each other. I met the jovial Vishnu who was chatting with one of the few men here bigger than Ramsey: Thor.

Hemsworth was prettier, but only about half the size of the giant god.

After that, Ramsey introduced me to a pleasant duo of women, both dressed conservatively: Nuwa and Ame-no-Uzume-no-Mikoto, Uzume for short. They were genial and kind, and I could feel the weight of their power, yet they didn't lord it over me.

Then we spoke to a pair of gods who looked sort of like identical twins: Belobog and Czernobog. Their features were the same, but one had extremely pale skin — almost luminous — with pure white hair. The other had onyx black skin and hair and emitted shadows.

As we made the rounds, I asked Ramsey if "*that* God" would be here and Ramsey nearly laughed himself hoarse.

Apparently, *He* didn't do these sorts of events, and his name was Yahweh if I ever did meet him.

Yet, some of the daemons of that pantheon — angels — were attending and Ramsey even pointed one out. He was the epitome of a warrior-angel: golden hair and wings, with golden armor worn over flowing white robes. We didn't talk to him.

I began to lose track of names and faces and then Ramsey spotted someone across the room and hurried me over to meet them.

"I think you'll get along well with her," Ramsey said as he got the attention of the other woman.

She wore a flowing cream-colored gown that was gathered up over one shoulder and flowed like silken waters over her full figure in a Grecian style. The diagonal cut meant her left breast was very much exposed, half a nipple showing above the fabric, which seemed to barely cling to her fullness. Long, wavy hair cascaded down to her thighs and seemed to shimmer through shades of autumn: umber brown, auburn, and dark-honey-gold, with highlights of fiery red. Her face was a perfect oval with high round cheeks, large amber eyes, and full, blushing lips, which smiled at me.

"Ana, meet Aphrodite... she's Grey's... ah... great grandaunt?" He looked to Aphrodite for confirmation.

"Oh! Hello!" she said, excited. "You must be the new goddess I've been hearing so much about!" She embraced me in a friendly way, kissing both of my cheeks. "And please don't call me great-grand-anything. If we're not directly related, let's just say we're all... cousins... yes?"

"Has Grey told you about me?" I asked as she drew back.

She laughed. "Grey doesn't talk to anyone about anything. He's rather tight-lipped. No, I have other ways of keeping track of things, especially when love and lust are involved. My many kids keep me appraised of such things... and here's one now!"

I turned and saw an embarrassed and blushing Harmonia approaching. "Ah... hello Mother," she said to Aphrodite.

"Have you been telling your mother about me?" I asked, not particularly accusing, mostly curious.

"A little," Harmonia said. "Though I think it's my brother Eros who's been telling most of the tales."

"Eros?" I asked, confused.

"You might know him better by his Roman name," Ramsey said. "Cupid."

Aphrodite giggled. "If people are falling in love, he keeps track of them... and you, my dear Ana, have been doing *a lot* of falling in love, haven't you?"

My cheeks heated. "Can Eros... ah... see us?" That seemed a bit pervy to me.

"Oh, yes," Aphrodite said, with a grimace. "He was the first voyeur. But don't worry, I'm the only one he tells things to. Your secrets are safe with me."

Yup, I was super-heated and blushing to my toes now. "Oh... good... thanks."

Aphrodite laughed. "Don't be embarrassed, dear! Love is a wonderful thing, and so is sex. From what I hear, they're your aspects as well, don't you agree with me?"

"I do," I said smiling, feeling just a little relieved.

"And don't worry," Harmonia said. "I only told my mother the more public details of your life, nothing private. We're friends. I wouldn't do that to a friend."

Thank the gods...

"Why, hello there! What a lovely trio of women. Dear Aunt Aphrodite, you must introduce me to this stunning creature!" This from a robust man as he approached.

He too was dressed in the Grecian style, a toga covering his girth, and he had a salt-and-pepper beard and flowing silver hair.

"Hello, Zeus," Aphrodite said, voice just a little strained. Then she whispered to me, "Watch out, he's an uber-lech. He'll sleep with anyone and anything in any form. Oh, and he loves his titles." She turned back to Zeus. "Your Most Royal Excellency! I'm sure you know my daughter, Harmonia. And this is Anais Baker, she's new, but alas, she's already spoken for."

Ramsey pressed close behind me, one possessive arm around me.

Zeus still eye-fucked me for a long moment while licking his lips.

"Too bad," he said a bit blatantly. Then, finally deeming to address me directly, he said, "You, my dear, are a truly fetching creature. It's so rare to meet a new goddess as lovely and ripe as you are."

Wow, could he hear himself? Super-creep much?

"Stop pestering the girl!" This from a new woman on the scene who began smacking Zeus with a scepter of some sort. I liked her instantly. She had a fuller, motherly figure, and was demurely draped in a deep blue dress. Her raven hair was done in an elaborate up-do, like a fountain, with falls of hair splashing down over her shoulders.

Zeus grumbled.

Aphrodite grinned. "Ana, meet Hera, Zeus' sister and wife."

"Ex-wife!" Zeus spat out, trying to swat Hera away.

"Since there aren't any lawyers that deal in divine

marriages, divorce among the gods is... subjective," Harmonia explained to me.

"It's a pleasure to meet you, my dear," Hera said, still happily bashing Zeus.

"I need to go get Horus," Ramsey whispered in my ear from behind. "Are you okay here?"

I nodded then turned my head to kiss him. Neither of us cared if people saw our display of affection. In fact, I thought Ramsey reveled in "claiming" me in front of these other gods. His kiss was deep and possessive and longer than I would have expected, not that I minded. And when he pulled away, I was left just a bit breathless.

Ramsey smiled and left with a wink.

"Ah... young love!" Aphrodite sighed, hand on heart.

"Young?" I scoffed. I was nearly forty and Ramsey was like... three thousand years old!

"Perhaps I should say... *new* love?" Aphrodite corrected herself.

"That would be more accurate, yes."

Zeus finally fled from Hera's barrage. "That's better, just us ladies now!" Hera said. "Shall we mingle a bit?"

"That would be lovely," I said with a smile and a nod.

Hera grinned. "Don't worry, we'll keep all the leches away and only introduce you to the prettiest, nicest, and most eligible gods."

"I'm spoken for," I said.

"Oh...? Ah... well, I guess it doesn't matter then," Hera said. "Still, come, this way, so many people to meet!"

As I followed Hera through the crowd, I caught sight

of another daemon who looked like an angel. This one wasn't wearing armor, just a flowing white robe, and his hair was more platinum blond, long and straight and silken. I couldn't see his face, but something about the man sparked a pull within me. I was... drawn to him.

Then, just as quickly as I'd glimpsed him, I lost sight of him.

"Who—?"

But Hera was pulling me toward another group, making introductions. The moment passed, and my curiosity faded as I met other fascinating gods.

ANAIS

"Make way for your most glorious host, His Excellency, the High and Most Royal God-King, Horus!" The voice boomed across the hall and everyone hushed for a moment.

I looked and saw Ramsey first, towering over most of the others nearby. The man next to him was opulently attired in far too much gold and gilt. His crown was a towering thing of red and white with a large golden snake emerging from the front, and his eyes scanned the crowd, haughty and superior.

"The only thing Horus is king of, is assholes," Hera said with a sniff. "He's nearly as bad as Zeus."

I laughed... just a little too loud... and it echoed across the silent hall, making all eyes turn to me, including Horus'.

"Who is this most enchanting woman?" Horus demanded, hurrying toward me as Harmonia, Aphrodite, and Hera formed a barrier in front of me.

Horus glanced at the three women as he drew near.

"If you three wish to join me in bed with this new woman, I would be happy to oblige you," he said with a cocky sneer. "But otherwise, let me through, so I might get to know my future bride!"

His gaze was all lusty possession. Zeus' eye-fucking had been blatantly sexual... but Horus' eyes were putting me in chains, claiming me, then defiling me, and I shivered with disgust.

"Stay away from her," Ramsey said, a crushing hand on Horus' shoulder, pulling him back. Ramsey then spun around to face the man putting himself between us.

Horus stepped to the side so he could see me again.

"Is this your new woman?" Horus asked with desirous awe. "I knew I'd have to have her. The tales haven't done her justice. Give her to me Ramsey or face my wrath."

He spoke as if I was something to be passed from man to man. What a dick. Hera was right, he was king of assholes for sure.

Ramsey didn't move. Instead, he gripped Horus' chin and forced his face up to look at Ramsey again.

"No. Fucking. Way." Ramsey's tone was scary. I'd never heard this level of outrage. "And I don't fear your wrath, cousin. You, however, should fear mine!"

I felt it then, Ramsey's strife being unleashed and pouring over everyone in the area.

Horus stepped back, tearing his face out of Ramsey's

grip. "I am The God King and I shall have what I desire! I claim it by Divine Right!"

Gods, this idiot was nothing more than a petulant child!

Ramsey's voice was deathly low, rumbling. "So be it. I challenge you to a Divine Duel!"

Everyone around us gasped.

I sighed out a long, "Fuck." I didn't even know what a Divine Duel was, only that everyone around me seemed to think it was a big deal.

"Ramsey, don't do this, I—" *can protect myself.* But I never got a chance to say it.

Ramsey spun around to face me. "You'd give yourself to him?" he demanded, his face contorted in rage-filled disgust.

Horus gave a victorious laugh.

"No," I said loud enough for everyone to hear. "But I *can* defend myself."

Ramsey blinked. "Right, yes, sorry, Ana." He came and knelt before me. "But please allow me to be your champion in this. I've been waiting for a chance to beat the snobby superiority out of my cousin for thousands of years."

I couldn't blame him.

I raised a hand, the gesture telling Ramsey to wait just a moment for my decision. Then I summoned my war and law, my shimmering armor forming around me, sword in hand as I strode over to Horus.

"You are a perverse and whiny child of a god. You'd

never be man enough for me, and if you ever get closer to me than we are now, I will cut you down, I swear it." My voice carried and echoed through the hall.

Everyone heard my oath, my vow, and power reverberated through me as it had when I'd confronted Ramsey's father.

"It's a good thing you'll be facing Ramsey and not me," I added, "as I'd likely cut off your tiny prick, assuming I could even find it."

That left Horus gaping.

I strode back to Ramsey, letting my armor vanish, my aspects fading. "Yes, you have my permission to be my champion in this silly duel, but don't kill the twit, just rough him up a little, understood."

Ramsey grinned. "I'll try to restrain myself." He rose and turned back to Horus. "Do you accept my challenge?"

Horus was clearly shaken, but he also seemed unable to back down. He slowly drew himself up to his full height... which was tall, but not as tall as Ramsey. "Yes!"

People began to move, and I rolled my eyes at the idiot.

Ramsey called out, "Maat! Draw us a circle!"

A woman stepped forward. She had beautiful dark skin and black feathery wings. As people moved aside, she began pacing out a circle, chanting as she went. Wherever she stepped, her footprints glowed to life and formed a golden line behind her.

Once she'd completed her circuit, a circle shone

brightly with golden light for a moment before dying down to a dull glow. Ramsey tossed aside his coat and shirt and stepped into the circle topless. His mountains of muscle heaved and bunched as he stretched and readied himself.

Horus didn't take anything off, stepping into the circle with quiet confidence. "You know you cannot resist my Word of Rulership," Horus said confidently. "You, who are nothing more than a half-breed. Your mother was mortal. My parents are both greater gods. You may be physically stronger, half-breed, but you're no match for me."

"Is that true?" I whispered to Harmonia.

She sighed. "Most of it is posturing, but there is some truth to his words. Ramsey's mother was mortal, but that doesn't mean much. Horus may be the son of two gods, older and inherently more powerful, but he's also a lazy git and didn't bother to practice his power. Whereas Ramsey has spent all of his shorter life making himself the best with his aspects."

Harmonia hedged for a moment, perhaps considering her next words. "Horus' main attack is his Word of Rulership, which is no joke. I honestly don't know if Ramsey is strong enough to overcome it. I'd give them roughly even odds."

"Oh." That surprised me. Horus looked so weak and insignificant compared to Ramsey. Now I was just a bit worried.

"I'm fifteen hundred years older than you are!" Horus

taunted. "You wouldn't even have been a king if not for my approval! And what a king you were. You oversaw the beginning of the end of Egypt's dominance! You were a fool then, and you're a fool now to challenge me." Horus laughed. "You only attained celestial status *after* your death, but I was born a god!" The petulant ass was reveling in his own words.

Ramsey barked a laugh, finally responding. "Exactly," he said, softly.

Horus balked, clearly wondering what he'd said wrong.

I hadn't caught it either, but Ramsey continued.

"You were born a god and people reluctantly accepted you because they had to. But I... I was *revered* as a mortal and it was the prayers of all of Egypt which made me a god. I was beloved of the people far more than you were. And as for the fall of Egypt, where were *you* during that time? If I recall correctly, you were off trying to seduce the goddess Sita, but she refused you at every turn. And since then, you've done nothing but jerk off and complain, while I've been building my power. We'll let this duel determine which of us is superior."

Horus was livid, red-faced with rage. He turned to the black-winged woman Maat. "Begin!" he shouted at her.

Ramsey settled into a fighting stance as Maat raised a hand, then let it fall.

Ramsey took two steps and then I felt it. The huge outpouring of power from Horus. Half the room was sent to their knees. I managed to stay on my feet, as did

Aphrodite and Hera, but Harmonia grunted and was forced down.

Ramsey was also affected, but not much, only slowed. He forced himself forward as if against a hurricane's wind.

So... *this* was Horus' power?

"What are Horus' aspects," I asked Aphrodite.

"Rulership and the heavens."

"The heavens?"

"He's a sky god, but it's less about the sky as it is about being... above everyone else. There are elements of wind and sunlight and moonlight, but mostly it's about the power of the unknown around us and above us."

"Oh."

I honestly had no clue how Ramsey would fare against such powers.

Horus was sneering, simply letting his power wash over everyone, enjoying how it made people kneel before him, although, as Ramsey stalked closer, Horus slipped nimbly to one side, getting farther away again with a laugh.

I understood now. This battle would end one of two ways. Either Ramsey would get to Horus and beat the man to a pulp, or Horus would exhaust Ramsey, forcing him to yield eventually.

I tried to reach out to Ramsey with my aspect of love and connect with him but something blocked me.

Maat stared at me, her eyes narrowed, and she shook her head slowly.

Apparently, her circle was keeping outside influence from affecting the match and she wasn't happy about me trying to help.

I nodded to her, understanding now.

So, I simply shouted. "You can do this, Ramsey. Crush that little prick!"

And, as if my words had indeed given him strength, Ramsey surged forward. He lunged and managed to get a meaty hand around Horus' scrawny arm before the man could flee again.

"Now you're mine!" Ramsey said viciously and punched Horus with his left hand. It was an offhand hit, but still, Ramsey's punch connected solidly with Horus' face and sent the man reeling. Horus seemed to bounce off an invisible wall at the edge of the circle and fall to his knees.

His power faded.

Ramsey pounced, driving a knee up into Horus' chin, and the smaller man flew back and bounced off the circle-barrier once more. This time, Ramsey caught him before he could fall, a thick hand around Horus' neck, and slammed him up against that invisible wall.

"Don't you *ever* treat Ana, or any woman, with such disrespect again!" Ramsey roared, punctuating his rant with punches.

Surely Horus would submit soon. I couldn't believe he could take much more of this. He seemed completely lifeless in Ramsey's grip.

Even Ramsey paused. I'd told him not to kill Horus, and perhaps he thought he was getting close.

Tension hung in the air as everyone watched the still scene.

Then, in a flash, Horus' arm shot up and he placed a hand on Ramsey's head. "Submit!" he slurred from a broken mouth.

The effect of that one commanding word drove Ramsey to his knees. The big man released Horus, seemingly crushed under some impossible weight.

"Submit!" Horus shouted again, spewing spittle and blood. Whatever was crushing Ramsey seemed to redouble and the large man flinched and was driven a little lower.

"Submit. Submit. Submit. Submit. Submit!" Horus roared. Every word drove Ramsey down, though each seemed less impactful than the last.

Ramsey was still on his knees, bent over with one hand on the floor. His aspect had been out and roaring with power since he'd first unleashed it before the fight, but it surged and strengthened in that moment.

The sheer power of the two competing aspects cracked the floor around Ramsey with a sickening crunch, indenting slightly. Then Ramsey surged back up, his hand going around Horus' neck again. They remained locked, with Horus' hand on Ramsey's head, and Ramsey's hand around Horus' throat. Their power thrummed and crashed together, and the room seemed to shimmer with the contest of wills.

Then Horus started twitching. His eyes began to bulge, legs kicking. His hand on Ramsey's head lifted away to scratch at Ramsey's arm, which was still tight around Horus' throat. He couldn't breathe, and he clearly knew he was about to lose this fight. The thrashing increased to a frenzy of limbs, then Horus went still.

The invisible wall vanished — the glowing circle of gold fading — as Ramsey pushed Horus outside the circle and released him. Horus fell, limp. Several gods and daemons went to check on him as Ramsey turned and stalked back to me.

"He's alive," Ramsey said, sounding just a bit rough himself.

"Thank you," I whispered. "He's an ass, but he doesn't deserve to die."

To that Ramsey just grunted.

In the next moment, Horus was up and stalking toward us.

"Little imp is persistent," Aphrodite muttered.

Horus stopped several paces away. "Ramsey can have you," he spat the words at me. "It's clear to me now, you're just a whore with no taste in men!"

I summoned my sword.

Horus yelped and stumbled back, falling on his ass.

I didn't put my sword away, didn't relent until Horus was scampering away. Gods and daemons laughed around us.

I sighed, vanishing my sword and shaking my head. "What a douche."

Ramsey chuckled as he put his shirt back on. "You can say that again."

"Ah... Anais?" Harmonia's tone was slightly curious, slightly scared.

I turned, seeing her, then followed her gaze to where the crowd was parting, letting something or someone through. Someone who was heading straight for us.

"Erini?" I breathed, but then those blocking my view fell away, and there, half-mad, with his wolf straining to get out, was Fen.

FEN

I was lost in a haze, reining in my beast with only a thread for a leash. With every speck of strength I had, I'd kept us moving toward Ana, fighting my wolf with each stumbling step. And I'd finally found her.

Even before I'd seen her, I'd felt her, like a beacon in my soul.

She called to me, pulled me, drove me. And here she was, finally, a vision in a black dress trimmed with blue and silver

Everything else around me was lost to madness, but her I saw clearly: radiant, beautiful, powerful, and compelling. The end of my quest.

Except seeing her brought no peace. My father's voice still boomed over and over in my head: *consume, destroy.* It was a command, a geas, and I'd resisted it as long as I could. I hoped just one word from Ana — whose voice usually calmed my beast — would override that of my father.

"Fen?" she gasped.

And there it was...

but it wasn't enough.

Loki was a powerful god, even if he rarely worked openly. His mental compulsions were insidious and insistent and not so easily dispelled.

"Fen? What's wrong? What can I do? What do you need?"

More words helped, and for a moment my beast was quelled to the point that I could take control, enough to utter one word.

"You."

My voice was rough and my canine mouth had trouble with the word, but it was clear enough.

"Right, come with me." She took my hand — my clawed and dangerous hand — and began leading me away. And my wolf let her.

My father's compulsion still pounded on me, but my wolf knew Ana well and apparently had decided that it could wait to consume and destroy until after whatever she had in mind.

We left the large ballroom and crossed a hall into a small room. She closed the door behind me. "Fen, I'm here for whatever you need."

She pulled me into a tight embrace. The feel of her lush body pressed against me was purely divine. Both my wolf and I agreed on that, and I was amazed at how easily she could love me, hold me, even though I was mostly wolf at the moment.

"Tell me what you need and I'll give it," she whispered intently.

The trouble was... I didn't know what I needed. I'd hoped her words would be enough to break me out of this trance, but my father's control remained. Her words had calmed my wolf enough that I could finally rest, just a little, no longer needing every ounce of my strength to hold it in check, but it still wasn't enough.

Ana pulled back. "Fen? Are you still in there? Say something."

"I'm here," I managed through my mangled mouth. "I'd hoped your words would help me, but I'm still struggling." As with many of my father's curses, I was compelled not to tell anyone what had happened. I hoped she understood.

She pulled me into another embrace. "I'm here, Fen." I felt her in my soul, filling me with her love. *I'm here. I'm here.*

It seemed she was at a loss for what to do as well, simply holding me and continuing to speak to me.

Ana, I love you so much. I'm sorry I ruined your evening. I... I can't tell you what happened, but I... my wolf... I don't know how much longer I can restrain it.

Even with my words?

Yes. They're helping, but... but my father's command

was too strong. Yet I couldn't tell her that. *I need... more than words?* I didn't even know what that meant... but she did.

You need me, she whispered into my soul. *Yes, one moment.*

She stepped back, reaching behind her neck to undo the top of her dress. Then she undid the clasps at her waist and the beautiful garment pooled on the floor. She stepped out of the dress and carefully laid it on a couch to one side of the room.

My wolf's appetite shifted from a hunger for destruction to a desire to mate, to consume this luscious creature before us. I didn't have nimble hands to work my clothes, so I tore what remained of my shirt and pants away with my claws. My cock sprang free as the tatters of my pants fell away.

"Oh, gods!" Ana gasped, eyes going wide.

I was mostly wolf at the moment and not-so-much man, and my raging cock reflected that, heavy and thick and reinforced with a rigid bone.

Her eyes flashed wide with fear. "Fen... I... oh wow.... Ah..."

But as I stalked toward her, she calmed, regaining her composure and speaking in soothing tones. "Yes, Fen, no matter your form, I'll always be here for you. Take what you must."

I reached her, clawed hands roughly grabbing her and turning her. I bent low, sniffing her pussy, smelling her heated readiness.

Ana, brace yourself, I warned her through our connection. *I'm barely in control.*

And I had a feeling Fenris The Destroyer did not mate pleasantly.

ANAIS

I surged my sex aspect as Fen's wolf surrounded me with its power. Huge clawed hands gripped my shoulders and he yanked me so my back was captured against his chest. His wolf's snout nuzzled into my hair, sniffing and snorting, and then, that oh-my-gods-sized cock pressed to my pussy.

The erection Fen sported at the moment put Ramsey's monster cock to shame. It was the largest dick I'd ever seen. I was a goddess of sex and could accommodate any man inside me, but *this* was no mere man.

So, I rammed my sex aspect down into my core, filling my pussy with searing liquid desire, and braced for Fen's entry.

There was no subtlety, no foreplay or easing in. His seeking tip found my swollen, wet and ready pussy, and with a swift jab, that world-ending cock pounded inside me all the way to the hilt, incredibly deep. Impossibly deep.

I cried out as I accepted him, formed to fit him as I'd hoped I would. Yet still, he was powerful and ferocious. With my sex surged, I felt every aching inch of him with pussy-clenching shocks of pleasure as he began vicious thrusting.

My arousal went from zero to a hundred in nothing flat, every cell in my body exploding with fiery bliss.

For just a moment my mind was completely and utterly blown away by this raw, animalistic sex. Ramsey sometimes liked it rough... but nothing like this. I didn't know if I'd get off from this hard and inhuman sex, but my aspect was doing everything in its power to make sure I enjoyed this as much as Fen did.

Throbbing heat coursed through me and pooled around my core, but even so, Fen was too much, too large, too hard, overwhelming. I grunted and groaned as he whined, his hands on my arms holding me tight, restraining me, keeping me in place so he could thrust harder, faster. My ass-cheeks would be sore tomorrow from his hips pounding into me, but I stayed with him.

I didn't know what he needed. When I'd been in his soul, I'd felt such turmoil mixed with his love. He'd also felt... suppressed, as if there were some other influence on him.

Fen, yes, take what you need, I'm here, I moaned into his soul.

I'm so sorry, Ana. His voice was so sorrowful and heartfelt, such a counterpoint to the savage fucking I was experiencing. *I... perhaps try surging your sex and love within me? Maybe that will help.* He seemed so lost and uncertain.

I did as asked. I pushed my sex into him, focusing on that mammoth cock, perhaps if he could just release, that would help?

At the same time, I pushed my love into him as well. I loved Fen, all of him, even this rough and vicious side of him. I took the bad with the good, and I knew he'd never hurt anyone willingly.

But then all my thoughts and my attention were cut off as Fen's already massive cock slammed into me fully... and swelled, like some cement-filled balloon at its base. My only lucid thought was to recall a documentary I'd seen about wolves and how they locked into place during mating.

Oh, Fuuuuuuuck...

All I felt was that pressure, solid and unmoving, planted inside me and pushing me past my limits as it pressed larger still. I let out a whine and so did Fen. Did this hurt him as much as it hurt me?

Except with the pain came an almost equal intensity of pleasure as my super-sensitive sheath pulsed around him. I'd never felt so filled by a man and the heady mix of agony and ecstasy shot through me with a surprise, powerful release.

I cried out, bucking and writhing even though I couldn't move much with Fen's hands and cock locking me in place. Pleasure roared through my veins, spinning me around and around and I couldn't catch my breath.

My orgasmic flood had nowhere to go as my pussy squeezed down hard on Fen's swollen cock, and then his wolf howled and a tidal wave of cum unleashed inside me.

I lost my mind at the extremity of pulsing pleasure, feeling his heat surge and fill me completely.

Yes Fen, take what you need! I gasped into him.

His inner voice was equally ragged and drawn, *Ana! Oh gods, Ana, I... I can't... It's so tight, and I can't stop. Gods!*

His wolf kept howling, a long and powerful cry into the night. Even as the knot of his cock swelled yet again and his release pounded even harder within me. I felt so full, so sated and stretched and...

Full...

Yes, full!

The realization hit me almost as hard as the unending orgasm pounding through me. Fen's wolf needed to consume, driven by a deep gnawing hunger, an emptiness that could never be filled.

Unlike Grey's void, which needed to be controlled, Fen's wolf needed to be filled.

I needed to make sure he was sated, fulfilled, whole.

I opened my sex up to the max, my stretched pussy pulsing around Fen's cock to make sure I drew out every last drop of his cum, while at the same time, I shunted all of my love into Fen's soul, filling him completely.

Then, to seal in my devotion, I put a vow of law on

both of us, binding us, filling him now and pledging I would always be there to fill him when he needed it.

The howl around me changed pitches, more contented, soothing, low and laden.

Yes! Fen shouted within me. *Yes, I can feel it. That did it. My wolf is receding! You did it, Ana!*

And slowly, as my sex drew out every aching ounce of Fen's release, that heavy knot inside me began to ease. As it did, I felt Fen return. His clawed hands became human and the nips of his teeth and the sniffing of that wolfen head shifted to soft kisses.

Still stuck together, we staggered to a couch and collapsed onto it, both on our knees. We leaned heavily against the back of the couch as Fen's wolf slowly faded and the wrecking ball inside me dissipated to the point that Fen could finally pull out from me. And like a cork being removed from a champaign bottle, when Fen's knot slid out, our combined releases finally burst forth. I groaned with relief and residual, tingling pleasure.

All I could do for a long moment was kneel there, still and gasping, as Fen tried to catch his breath beside me.

"Ah... sorry about that..." he breathed, blinking at the mess I was making... that he'd caused.

I shook my head. "Don't be sorry. We needed to do that. If not now, then at some point. It was the only way to satisfy your wolf, for now and forever." Even if it had been a bit... extreme. I'd be sore and walking funny for a month... or until I healed myself. Speaking of which, I began to mend my stretched and strained bits.

"Yeah," he whispered. "I can feel it. My wolf is almost... purring inside of me." He gave a breathy laugh. "Apparently all it takes to fill me, is to fill you."

I chuckled as well.

"Would you be a dear and get me something to clean up with?" I asked.

I hadn't had time to take in the space when we'd entered, so I did now. The room was a private sitting area with a couple of large couches and chairs and a few side tables. It also had a small, two-piece bathroom by the door.

"It looks like there's an ensuite." I tilted my head to indicate where.

Fen rose to do as I'd asked when the door to the hall burst open, flying off its hinges and nearly hitting Fen as it shot past him.

There, in the doorway, was a small, sturdily built woman with dark hair and tanned skin. Raw hatred and savage loathing burned in her eyes when she looked at me.

"You tried to steal my Fenris, didn't you?" she spat. "Well, you can't have him. He's mine!"

So... *this* was Erini.

And before I could do anything, she unleashed all of her envious, vengeful fury on me.

ANAIS

Erini's blast of destructive fury never reached me. Fen stepped in front of me and devoured it in one gulp.

"Get out of here!" he shouted at me. "I'll take care of her!"

My first thought was: *like hell, I can fight too!*

But then Fen and Erini went at it, full-force and furious. Fen brought forth his beast enough to match Erini blow for destructive blow, but that quickly led to the small room being torn apart. It started to collapse on the two of them

My second thought was: *I need to make sure no one else gets hurt, but I can't get past Erini.* She was blocking the only doorway.

Then a stray blast of her fury destroyed a wall nearby making a new exit.

"I'm going to make sure everyone else evacuates, then I'll come back and help," I called back to Fen as I climbed through the hole. Fen was too preoccupied to respond.

I bolted for the door of the next room... but with my hand on the knob, I realized I was still buck naked.

I summoned my armor, shimmering around me. It didn't entirely obscure my form, but it did more than some of the dresses other goddesses had been wearing tonight. It would have to do.

I ran into the hall, but Erini was still in the doorway of the other room. She screeched her hatred and blasted a blazing line of energy at me.

With a yelp, I ducked back into the room I'd just left, then quickly dove back out and rolled across the hall to another door, bursting through it and into the main ballroom.

Some people were already fleeing from the rumbling and blasting nearby, and I shouted, using all the command presence I could summon through my law aspect.

"Get out of here! Two daemons of destruction are going at it, and I don't know how long things will hold!"

That got their attention and people began running. Most headed for the exits, though a few ran toward the fight or toward me. Ramsey and Harmonia headed in my direction. But even as they did, Erini burst into the large room and let out a terrible bellow of pure fury.

Pain lanced through my skull and I covered my ears, watching as the ceiling and floor both shattered from the sound wave. My pulse racing, I dove for safety, but

Ramsey and Harmonia weren't fast enough and fell through the collapsing floor.

"No!" I shouted, reaching out in vain toward my lover and my friend, but they were gone into the blackness below. Then heavy chunks of the ceiling crashed past me into the hole and on top of them.

Cement dust billowed around me, obscuring my vision and clogging my lungs. I wanted to go after Ramsey and Harmonia... or destroy Erini... but I couldn't do either at the moment, and right now, I just needed to get somewhere where I could breathe.

I heard more sounds of fighting as I staggered to my feet, coughing. Then the floor dropped out from under me, tilting, and I fell, sliding down a level.

I landed on my feet in a mostly cleared area, and bolted, before more of the floor above me came crashing down.

Frantic, I swept my gaze around trying to find Ramsey or Harmonia, but I couldn't see anything except rubble.

"Ramsey! Harmonia!" I had to find them.

Concentrating, I reached out through my love aspect, connecting with all three of my guys. Fen was strained and struggling but alive, while Grey was still at his apartment. With Erini here, I knew my kids were safe so I reached out to him quickly.

Erini is here. We need you, I said into his soul.

Coming, he replied, sending a ripple of relief washing through me.

I turned my attention to Ramsey. He was somewhere far below me and I sensed a crushing pain from him.

So far down!

There was no way I could get to them.

I could only pray he and Harmonia could get themselves out... though perhaps I could help... in another way.

RAMSEY

I GROANED IN THE DARK.

The crash and roar of more destruction echoed somewhere far above me.

It felt like the entire building had fallen on me, driving me, and the floors beneath me, down and down into darkness.

Every inch of me was in pain and the warmth on my face and leaking out of far too many parts of my body told me I was slowly bleeding out.

But... I was a daemon prince and wouldn't die that easily. I was also the Lord of Strife and made to keep going even when conflict had beaten me down.

And in times like this, when the physical limits of my body couldn't help me, my chaos would sustain me. It wouldn't heal me, but it would help me keep going, help me survive, and help me get out from under the press of thousands of tons of concrete.

I groan-cried as my chaos surged around me. Slowly — since most of what lay on top of me were huge pieces of debris — things moved, and my chaos created an area around me, removing the crushing concrete.

That gave me a chance to crawl to my knees and assessed myself. One leg had been crushed, but with my supernatural toughness, it was mostly just a mass of bruises, perhaps a fracture? I could walk on it, but I'd be limping. The other leg was sore all over, but otherwise strong enough to support me.

There was also a wound on my side where a piece of rebar had stabbed into my abdomen. I tore up what remained of my jacket and tied it around me, staunching that wound. My arms were beaten and bruised but mostly well. My right arm had been crushed a bit more and probably wouldn't be able to do anything too strenuous, and my head ached, pounding with a thousand sledgehammers. I'd removed the tons of concrete trying to crush my skull, but the effects of that pressure hadn't fled.

Slowly, I moved, letting my chaos cut away the debris around me. Things shifted and fell and crashed in the hole I left behind me, but I tried to be careful. I'd seen Harmonia fall near me, and could only pray I was moving in her direction.

I found her in a mostly open pocket of debris, but she'd taken a beating and wasn't quite as tough as I was. She was unconscious, blood covered her head and torso, and both of her legs were trapped, crushed.

"Fuck," I whispered.

I tried to lift the concrete laying on her lower half, but my arms were near to useless. So, I urged it carefully away with a bit of my chaos, freeing her.

Harmonia groaned, which was good. It meant she was still alive.

I moved her carefully, picking her up in my weary arms. She, at least, I could carry.

"Ramsey," she muttered through broken lips.

"I'm here, I'll get us out."

"I... used my harmony to try to still the collapse, but... ohhhhh... everything hurts."

I nodded. "Don't talk."

She leaned against my chest, resting in my arms, as I continued to burrow through the debris with my chaos.

Then, finally, I managed to emerge into a dark hallway, perhaps a sub-basement of the hotel. There were no lights, but my celestial nature meant I could still make out the form of things, if only barely. Once there, and no longer needing my chaos — and fearful it might cause this still-standing area to collapse — I let it go.

But with my chaos went the last of my strength, and I staggered to one knee, setting Harmonia down carefully. I could hardly move, let alone carry her, and had to lean against the wall to catch my breath and regain some strength.

The trouble was, even if I managed to regain some strength, how in hell was I going to get out of here... and get Harmonia out with me?

"Ana," I breathed, desperate. "I need you!" I needed her strength, her love, her determination, and her healing. "Ana," I huffed again. "Please!"

Ramsey?

The simple sound of her voice within me caused me to break down and I wept tears of relief.

Ana? Yes. I'm here.

And Harmonia?

She's with me, but she's hurt.

And you? Concern filled the soft inner voice of hers.

I'll survive. It wasn't a blatant lie. I just didn't want her to worry. So I changed the topic. *I don't know where I am or even if there's a way out. I'm safe enough for now, but if any more of the building collapses...* I didn't want to think about what would happen.

I was planning on stopping the fight that was causing that. But do you need me first? she asked. *Do you want me to come for you?*

No, go. Stop this. But... is there any way you could lend me a bit of strength? If I can walk and carry Harmonia, I might be able to find a way out on my own. I can gain strength from my conflict, but... I don't want to summon it for fear of it causing more damage down here.

I felt her pensive tension as she considered my request.

Let me try something, she said, sounding uncertain.

Slowly, the hall around me seemed to dissolve. The darkness faded to a dull haze of grey and then a bright, radiant light in the form of a woman appeared in the gloom. And though her form was obscured in brilliance, her face was clear to me.

Ana.

"Ramsey?" She beamed. "It worked!"

"Ana? Where are we?" I asked. Looking down, I could see an ephemeral version of my body through the haze. I, too, was glowing, but not as brightly as Ana.

"In your soul. I thought if I could speak to you in your soul, perhaps I could visit you there as well."

She floated toward me, ethereal arms reaching out, her hands finding my face. She drew me close, her lips finding mine in a soft kiss, and through that connection, I *felt* her.

It was more than just a kiss, more than a linking of consciousnesses, but an abiding hold on my soul, binding me to her. And through that bond, came strength and power. I felt revitalized once more.

I gasped as she drew back, smiling.

"How was that?" she asked, voice breathy.

"Best kiss ever," I breathed.

"Then this will be even better."

She enfolded me in her arms, in her light, and I felt her warmth and the soft press of her against me. This time, when her lips teased mine, we seemed to merge, our bodies melting together. It was the most intimate experience of my very long life.

I was deeper inside her than any physical thrust could manage, and she was inside me as well. More than her presence... I felt her aspects flowing around me: her love, and — far more important right now — her healing.

Distantly, I sensed my body mending and my strength returning.

I was so caught up in this transcendent ecstasy of connection, I whispered, "I love you, Ana."

She giggled. "I know. I can feel it."

And... "I feel your love as well," I breathed. It was an amazing revelation to be exposed to all her glorious brilliance and devotion.

"I need to go," she whispered, her light beginning to fade. "But call me again if you can't find a way out from where you are."

"I will. I love you, Ana."

She filled me with her love one last time, even as my awareness returned to my body. *I love you too,* her voice echoed in my soul.

I breathed a heavy, long breath as I came to myself.

Feeling strong and refreshed, I lifted Harmonia.

She groaned.

"Stay still, I've got you," I told her. "I'll get us out of here."

She gave a faint nod, mostly limp in my arms.

I moved forward with care through utter darkness until a flickering exit sign came into view down another long hall.

"Thank the gods," I breathed.

When I reached the stairs, they only went up. We were on the lowest possible floor of the hotel. I started up, counting basement levels as we passed them, but when we got to what should have been the first floor, a cave-in had crushed the stairs above us and the doorway out.

Heavy slabs of concrete were held precariously above us by the set of stairs leading up, and it looked like it might give way any moment. Even healed as I was, and strong as I was, I didn't think I could physically lift that much collapsed concrete, especially not while holding Harmonia.

That left only one option.

I whispered to Harmonia. "I'm going to use my chaos to make a hole." I'd never had someone with me inside my chaos before, I figured I should warn her.

"If you need it," she mumbled. "I can use my harmony to help balance your chaos."

"No, save your strength," I said. "I can do this."

Or so I hoped.

I wasn't sure how much chaos I'd need to burrow through this rubble, but if it was too much... I might lose control like I had in Queens.

I couldn't let that happen, not with Harmonia in my arms.

This was it, my ultimate test.

I summoned my strife. It tore at me, wanting to be let loose as I expanded the swirl of chaos to tear at the debris around us.

"Gods, this is terrifying," Harmonia whispered.

Welcome to every damned day of my life.

I summoned more and more chaos to tear away at the

massive slab of concrete blocking our path. It was slowly shredded into smaller and smaller bits, but the doorway still hadn't been uncovered.

With a roar, I pushed my chaos to its limits. That did it, the concrete was blasted away and so was the door, but beyond was only more rubble. I waited for my chaos to consume me... but it didn't.

I couldn't believe it. My strife was blasting through me, but I was still calm and in control. Seeking within myself, I was surprised to find a part of Ana had remained within me. I felt her abiding and enduring love. She soothed the tempest in my soul and grounded me, steadied me. Because of her, I could fully summon my chaos without losing control.

I love you, Ana! My goddess, my savior! I sang into my soul.

Then I pushed onward, moving through the rubble, step by slow and careful step, blasting the debris away until we finally stepped out to find the night's sky above us.

I released my strife as we left the debris behind. Even with Ana's stabilizing influence, keeping my chaos controlled and at its max for so long had taken its toll on me. I fell to one knee, having to put Harmonia down.

"That was the most amazing and frightening thing I've ever experienced," she breathed.

Amazing and frightening? Yeah, that was me to a tee.

ANAIS

After I finished with Ramsey, I found a set of stairs and ran up into the lobby of the hotel.

"Everyone out!" I shouted at the milling mass of people who seemed to be staggering around in shock.

They began to run, even as heavy cracks formed in the ceiling above me, spider-webbing out far too quickly and raining down small bits of plaster.

"Fuck," I breathed and sprinted for the door, as heavier chunks began to fall.

A large fragment of the ceiling broke free above me. I tried to leap out of the way, but I wasn't fast enough.

Oh gods, no...

Then time seemed to slow.

There was a flurry of white around me, a silken fall of platinum hair, the fluff of feathers, and strong arms enfolded me. I winced, my eyes shut, and hoped...

I heard the crash of the ceiling but didn't feel

anything, and an eerie, deathly quiet rang in my ears. I risked a peek, but all I saw was a greyish haze.

"Anais?"

The voice was smooth and soft, and an angelic face looked down at me. Behind him, his wings were torn and bloodied, and bits of the shattered ceiling lay around us.

I blinked my other eye open. It was the angel with platinum hair I'd seen earlier, the one I'd been drawn to.

He'd saved me?

Also... he'd said my name.

"Who are you?" I asked, before choking on dust and coughing for half a minute.

The man placed a hand on my shoulder and smiled. Warmth flowed into me and my lungs cleared and the aches and pains of my body faded. At the same time, his wings mended, returning to pristine white.

"Is that better?" he asked.

I nodded. "Thank you."

"To answer your question, my name is Raphael." A soft strange looked filled his striking silver-blue eyes. "And I'm your father."

I gaped, eyes wide, not understanding, even as everything sank in. His hair... silver and silken... like mine. His eyes were the same silver blue. Even some of his facial features, something around the sumptuous lips and at the edges of his eyes, matched my own.

But... No...

He was an angel!

And I was... a goddess. My mother had been a goddess.

Mother... goddess

Father... angel.

It took far too long for my mind to make sense of all this.

"Fuck me," I whispered. Then I realized what I'd just said in front of my father and stammered... "Ah... no, I mean, I... Fuck... How...?"

Raphael laughed. "Sorry, I know that was a lot to dump on you when you've already been through so much tonight."

He looked me over, but it wasn't the usual scan most men gave me. Instead, there was a note of curiosity and confusion in this look.

"You've found your divinity? How? That wasn't supposed to happen," he half mumbled to himself, then huffed as if to clear his thoughts. "You're just as much a mystery to me as I must be to you. I'm sorry, Anais, I wish I had time to talk, but I need to help the wounded." He helped me to my feet and we gingerly made our way through the lobby out into the fresh night air.

In the distance, I could hear more crashing and the sounds of fighting.

"My friends, they're still in there. I need to help them!"

I'd somehow spirit-healed Ramsey, but he and Harmonia — who was still injured — were in there somewhere, far below everything. Could they get out?

And Fen...

"You're as brave as your mother," Raphael said with a sad smile.

"Inanna?"

"Yes. I'd ask how you know," he said, "but that's a conversation for another time."

I narrowed my eyes at him. "And you're not going to stop me from going back in there?"

"I couldn't stop your mother, so I'm assuming I can't stop you."

A man who knew his place, I liked that in a father.

He motioned to the various injured humans, daemons, and gods all around us. They were laid out in the street or staggering to get farther from the damaged building. "I'll stay here and heal those I can."

I looked at the sea of bloodied and wounded people and my heart clenched. I had the aspect of healing, too... I should help them.

But that would take too long and I needed to get back inside. I had to pick one or the other.

Or maybe not? Maybe I could do both?

I'd just healed Ramsey from a distance... but I was pretty sure that had been because I'd been connected to him through my aspect of love.

Could I do that with others?

Fuck it, I had to try!

First, I summoned my love, reaching out with sympathy and caring to all of the wounded around me. I felt their spirits, felt the love within them, and connected to that.

Then...

I gathered my healing aspect and let it flow through that connection to everyone around me. It took more energy to heal someone if you weren't touching them — as I'd discovered with Ramsey — but I pushed myself, in hopes of healing as many as I could.

And mending the wounds for the dozens of people around me did indeed drain me. I stumbled, falling to my knees, unable to stay standing...but also unable to stop.

I reached out with love, connecting to more, pouring my healing into everyone I could, the need to heal *all* of them compelling me to test my limits. I put everything I had, everything I was, into healing these people.

But too many were hurt. I collapsed to my hands with the strain, crying out, then gritted my teeth and forced myself to keep going.

It was too much, and for a moment, I felt all of their pain, every injury lancing through me, and nearly passed out. Only then did I release my power and collapse, tears streaming down my face as I sucked in heavy breaths.

I couldn't believe it. I'd healed hundreds of people at once, but I'd still not been able to reach everyone, and more were coming out of the hotel as the fight raged inside.

I needed to stop Erini. Put an end to this fight before she caused more damage.

"Anais?" Raphael whispered beside me as he placed a

hand on my back, sending his soothing healing into me and restoring part — but not all — of what I'd lost.

I pushed myself up, then sat back on my heels. "I'm... good."

I dragged my attention to the hotel and saw Aphrodite helping someone I didn't know escape from the wreckage.

"What's it like in there?" I asked her as she drew near.

"Chaos," she said. "A few gods and daemons are trying to stop the two destroyers, but their attacks are only adding to the devastation and collapsing the building faster."

"Great," I said with a grimace. If I was going back in there, I'd need some way to keep myself from being crushed. I turned to my father. "What did you do to keep the ceiling from squishing us in there?" I asked.

"I used my aspect of peace to create an area of stillness around us. It kept most, but not all of the debris from falling on us." I'd seen his wings after, torn and bloodied, but I guessed that was better than crushed and dead. Also, he could heal and...

Wait...

Aspect of peace?

Even as I thought of it, I was filled with a deep well of serenity.

Peace!

Of course!

"Ah, Anais? You're... glowing," my father said in awe. "I can feel soothing power flowing off of you."

"I just found *my* peace," I murmured.

Slowly, I rose, feeling this new aspect fill me with a calm readiness for what I had to do, a new tool to help stop Erini's destructive madness. "I need to go."

Raphael didn't question me at all. He simply nodded, and I could see in his silver eyes that he knew I could do it, that he trusted me.

"Go," he whispered. "I'll stay here and help these people." I began to move away when another whisper caught my attention. "You're far stronger than I am anyway."

Was I?

Yes, I was.

And it was time to end this senseless destruction.

I strode back toward the ravaged building. Dust billowed out, and I couldn't see anything past a few feet, but I could hear the fighting.

Filled with determination, I marched through the rubble-strewn lobby and made my way down ruined and darkened halls.

"You," a rasping voice whispered. "You did this, didn't you?"

I turned to see Horus limping out from the shadows. His eyes were wide with delusion and delirium. He didn't look good: blood on his face, one of his arms hanging useless. His one leg looked like it had been half-crushed.

"Fuck," I whispered. Then louder. "You need to get outside and get healed."

He was an asshole, but he didn't deserve to die here. I

strode over to him, intending to heal him a little and help him toward the exit. But when I reached him, his good arm snaked out to my throat.

Eyes wild with lunacy, he croaked the word, "Submit!"

A crushing pressure drove down on me, but I didn't buckle, didn't fall to my knees. I resisted.

I'd been the one to approach him, so my oath to "cut him down" if he got too close hadn't kicked in. It did now. My war aspect surged, bringing my sword to my hand. I lifted the blade until it was pressed to his throat, my threat clear, even though I couldn't speak to voice it. Defiance danced in my eyes.

"Submit!" Horus tried again, harder, his power slamming into me, but it crashed uselessly against me, like a wave against rocks.

I lifted my sword another inch and drew blood from his neck.

"Fuck!" he hissed, letting me go and staggering back. "What's wrong with you, bitch?"

He had the nerve to ask that?

I regained my breath and my voice quickly, a touch of healing going a long way. "Either you get out of my sight this instant, or I'll end you, you sick, fucking bastard." I raised my sword again, the point near his shoulder.

He yelped and fled.

One minor annoyance dealt with, now to see to the major threats of the night.

Carefully, I made my way through the rubble, getting closer and closer to the sounds of fighting and chaos.

Except no matter how I squinted or concentrated, I couldn't quite make out exactly where people were. The darkness, mixed with the heavy fog of concrete dust filtering through the air, was too thick, and I had no idea what I was walking into despite being able to feel the presence of several daemons and gods.

I needed a plan. And one that didn't involve blindly walking into a fight between a god and goddess of destruction.

ANAIS

THE ONLY PLAN I COULD COME UP WITH WAS TO GET ERINI and Fen away from the building and out into the park.

Somehow.

The damage they'd done to the hotel — whether inadvertent or not — was catastrophic. I couldn't let them do any more, and I didn't want to put any other buildings at risk.

I stopped my forward march toward the battle and mentally reached out to Fen. *How are you, my love? Do you think you can lure Erini out to the park?*

Fen's voice, when he answered within me, was ragged. *I've tried several times to lure her away. But she seems fixated on you. It's all I can do to keep her away from you and others. I'm...* I felt and heard his pained hesitation. *She's too powerful. I'm struggling. I'm sorry, Ana.*

Don't be, my love. I'm here now and ready. Let me take the fight from you.

He didn't respond in words, but the relief I felt flooding through him was confirmation enough that he needed help. Fen was strong, but Erini, it seemed, was stronger.

"Erini!" I shouted. "If you want me, come and get me! I'll be in the park waiting for you."

"I'll kill you, bitch!" she screeched from somewhere ahead of me, her cry bellowed out from the chaos and darkness.

Quickly, I shifted into my dove form and flew out from the hotel toward Central Park. There was still a risk of inadvertent casualties outside, but the destruction level should decrease significantly in that more natural setting.

Still, I hoped and prayed I could keep this goddess contained as much as possible.

As I landed in a thicket at the edge of the park and returned to my human form, I summoned all my aspects.

War reinforced me, strengthening my armor, giving me my sword and bringing forth some minions to aid me. Love bolstered me, feeling my guys all alive and striving. Peace calmed me. Sex and fertility... weren't so useful... but they were there just in case. And law, I used my sense of justice to make sure the battle I was about to fight would be a righteous one.

Last, my healing surged through me, strengthening and reinforcing me, making sure I was at peak health for the fight to come.

Erini, like a fireball — blazing with a blood-red aura — blasted out of the hotel and hurtled toward me.

"Come at me, bitch," I whispered, thinking I was ready for whatever she might throw at me.

I was wrong.

With a horrid shriek, she unleashed not one but dozens of bolts of raw fury down on me.

My minions were blasted to nothingness in the blink of an eye. I tried to dance out of the way, avoiding her attack, but there were too many bolts and as fast as I was, I wasn't fast enough.

One crushing blast hit me, then another, tearing at my armor and my very essence. Relentless anger and jealous rage pounded through my soul as vengeful destruction pummeled me physically.

My armor protected me, preventing major damage, but I felt like I was bouncing around inside it, bruised and disoriented. My mind spun, trying to catch up and anticipate, but she was just too much all at once.

Erini laughed. "How'd you like that, little bug?"

Ana! I heard the twin cries within my soul almost at the same time before Erini's barrage suddenly lessened in intensity.

I dodged the few remaining bolts coming my way, catching a glimpse — through trees and the constant rain of dirt and debris around me — of Ramsey, sheathed in swirling chaos, attacking Erini.

Fen was limping toward me as well, adding his own all-consuming blasts.

That's my guys!

Keep her occupied for a moment, I have an idea, I sent to them.

Will do, Silverlocks, came Ramsey's reassuring bass.

I'll do what I can, Fen replied, sounding rough. He needed healing.

I shifted into my dove form and easily swooped through and around the blasts, then surged up into the sky.

"Where did you go, little bug?" Erini hiss-shouted.

Good, she didn't know where I was. She'd probably sense me in a moment, but would hopefully be distracted just long enough for me to...

I reached where I wished to be, above Erini, then I returned to myself, falling on her from behind, my sword slashing down.

She sensed me and shifted just in time. My strike, which had been aimed for the middle of her back, hit her shoulder... and severed her arm.

I shifted back to a dove as Erini screamed in pain and fury. She was preoccupied, at least for a moment, so I quickly darted down to Fen, returned to my human form, and healed his injuries. After everything else I'd been through tonight, I was feeling the pull of fatigue, but I was also filled with the thrill of battle, which kept me going.

"You're amazing," Fen breathed. His physical wounds were closed, but he was clearly still weak and tired.

"She's recovering!" Ramsey hissed, drawing near.

There was something different about him, a new strength and confidence, and then it hit me. I could feel his chaos unleashed and whipping around him, but it was also perfectly contained and controlled, far different from before.

"You good?" I asked as I rose.

"Better than ever."

"And I'm feeling up for a second round," Fen said standing next to me on the other side.

"Then, let's do th— ahh what the fuck?" My confidence wavered as I looked up at Erini.

Something was happening. She was shaking, vibrating, almost as if she was tearing apart from the inside... and it turned out... she was.

Throwing her head back with a scream of rage, she broke apart and shifted. Two more heads sprouted from her neck, and four more arms from her sides as she became all three furies in one body. A spiked whip appeared in one of her hands, a sword in another, and a shield in a third.

"Really?" I shouted as I summoned my sword and shield as well.

"You can't stop me!" her three heads said at once in a strange reverberating echo. "You've corrupted my brother and stolen my true love. Time to die, little bug!"

She came at us in a blur, all flailing arms and weapons and fury, screaming incoherently.

Ramsey lashed out with chaos, but she blocked with her shield.

Fen launched himself at her with tooth and claw, but her whip flashed out and caught him around the neck, flinging him away.

I fought her sword to sword, but I was being driven back by the storm of her rage.

I'd thought myself good with a sword, but that had been against mindless zompires. Against a trained goddess, I was losing... badly.

She was too fast. Her strikes slid past my guard and shattered my armor. Stabs and slashes opened my flesh, faster than I could heal them.

My armor remade itself only to be torn open again and again. Even with Fen and Ramsey distracting her, it wasn't enough. She was fury incarnate and she was winning.

Then, even as she continued her physical assault, another barrage of her fiery bolts surged out from her, surprising us.

Ramsey screamed, Fen was knocked back, and I was sent sprawling, armor blasted open, chest charred, the breath knocked out of me.

It would take me a moment to heal myself, but that gave Erini time to play. She went to Fen, kneeling beside him, one of her free hands fondling his face.

"We could have ruled it all — ruined it all — my prince of destruction," she moaned at him. Then she slapped him, hard, turning his head, before gripping it again and digging her nails in. "But no! You fucked that whore! You chose a nice pair of tits over your soulmate in destruction and for that, you'll die!"

Healing coursed through me, my armor mending. I sat up, slowly, still aching and wounded. I'd be ready in a moment... I just didn't know if Fen had that long.

Luckily Erini was still ranting. "All my life I've been told to rein in my rage, only bring it out a little at certain times. Well, fuck that! I've waited for so long to unleash my full power and now that I have, I *like* it! The world will burn, and you'll burn with it! It's time this world felt the wrath of the furies!"

I was up.

Ramsey had also staggered to his feet.

"Go to Hel," Fen spat at Erini.

"Been there. Born there. I'm all the worst that *is* hell and Hades," she responded, then lifted her sword over him.

"No!" I cried out, hoping to get her attention as I launched myself at her. I managed to get my sword between hers and Fen, blocking her blow. But that left me defenseless and one of her free hands backhanded me so hard, I was sent flying once again.

I landed hard, skidding over the ground, though my armor protected me for the most part.

Ramsey came at her next, his conflict spinning about him.

Erini smiled at him, extending one arm, and somehow siphoned off his chaos into her outstretched hand. She drank in his strife like it was the sweetest nectar, draining him of his aspect while strengthening herself, because strife and conflict were simply the end result of hatred, rage, and jealousy.

Ramsey, devoid of his chaos, staggered a few steps, then fell on hands and knees, gasping for breath.

Erini laughed, triumphant. When I groaned, rising again, one of her heads whipped around to face me, glaring daggers.

"You!" she spat. Turning back to Fen, she hissed, "I'll come back for you, once I've finished off your whore." Then she punched him so hard he went limp.

I cried out, but Erini only smiled and darted over to Ramsey as I struggled to my feet. She banished her weapons so all five arms could pummel him with rapid precision before I could even take a step. Without his chaos as defense, Ramsey was left broken and groaning on the ground.

"No!" I whimpered, summoning my war: my armor, sword, and shield yet again.

Erini stalked toward me, fury whipping around her, envious ire burning in her eyes. She was at the pinnacle of her power and I... suddenly had no clue how I was going to defeat her.

She stopped half a dozen paces from me, summoning her weapons and shield again, even as fiery bolts appeared in her two free hands. All three faces were grinning, all six eyes triumphant. "Who will save you now, little bug?"

ANAIS

E<small>RINI LET FLY HER BOLTS.</small> I <small>TRIED TO TOSS MYSELF OUT OF</small> the way, but she was too close and the bolts were too fast and they both—

Hit Grey as he put himself between me and the devastating attack. He was thrown back, crashing through the brush next to me, and Erini blinked, confused and stunned.

I had an opening and I should have attacked Erini, but I couldn't. I threw myself at Grey instead.

Don't be dead! I mentally begged.

He groaned, writhing on the ground, a large gaping hole in his chest. His muscles were gone and his ribs were exposed, cracked and charred. He was alive, but even with all his daemonic powers, I didn't know how long he might survive after a hit like that.

I couldn't risk losing him, so I knelt next to him and touched his shoulder to heal him. The wound began to close, but only a trickle of my power seeped into him before Erini was on us.

"Zaggy?" she whispered, her voice ragged. "What did you do, brother? Why would you protect this woman? I didn't mean to..." The pitch of her voice rose with every sentence, her madness escalating. "You," she snarled at me, drawing out the word, pouring all her vitriol and hatred into that one syllable. "You did this!"

Yeah... I was in for it now.

I rose, surging all my aspects. Healing pulsed through me, strengthening me. War sent every possible tactic to my mind, and Law reinforced war since I was on the side of justice and order. I didn't know if my peace and love and sex and fertility would be of any use, but they were all at the ready.

"You want me? Here I am," I muttered. "Let's do this, woman to woman, no bolts of destruction, just you and me, fighting it out to the end."

Erini's six eyes literally blazed with blood-red hellfire.

"Yes," she hissed, her voice seeming to echo within itself.

Stratagems swirled in my head. How did one beat a superior foe? A wise warrior needed to use cunning tactics or favorable battlefields to win. This field of battle was far from favorable, which meant all I really had was cunning.

"Fen, no don't!" I shouted, eyes going wide, looking behind her.

Erini half turned, only to find Fen wasn't there at all. I

flew in and struck while she was distracted, lopping off another of her arms.

Erini screamed. I had the advantage now and slashed again, but some natural defense mechanism of hers kicked in. A pulse of energy billowed out from her, pushing me away, and slamming me into a tree.

Three sets of fiery eyes slowly turned toward me. One of her heads was so crazed it was frothing at the mouth.

Well, Fuck.

She flew in and I blocked her whip with my shield, but then she was on me, two arms grasping my shield and pulling it away from me. Her sword swung in and cut through my armor into my side. At the same time, she bashed a fist into my face, hitting like a jackhammer.

I swung with my sword, but her one free hand stopped my arm, crushing my wrist before wrenching my arm the wrong way.

Agony, like nothing I'd ever felt before, exploded through my arm as joints were torn out of their sockets and tendons snapped. Then... just to be safe, she did the same thing to my other arm.

I screamed an inhuman sound.

Erini laughed.

"That's more like it," she snarled and she punched me in the face again, caving in my mouth. I couldn't scream anymore, choking on blood.

Erini finally had me at her mercy and she reveled in her hatred, bashing her fist over and over into my face.

"Let's see if anyone wants you once I'm done with you, little slut," she bellowed.

She was too close to use her sword and whip effectively, but her arms were doing a good job of pummeling the rest of me as well, breaking through my armor.

My healing couldn't keep up. Blood flowed over my chin from a shattered mouth and broken nose. I could barely see out of one eye, the other swollen shut, and my mind was growing hazy.

Then, thankfully, the punching stopped... only to have two of her hands shift up to grab my neck and squeeze.

I managed to gasp in one gulp of air... then... I was scrambling to breathe.

My arms hadn't mended, so I kicked at her. But she blocked my feeble attacks, then stabbed her sword into my legs until they were useless. And that was it. I had nothing left. My guys were down. No one was going to save me now, except me, and I'd done all I could. Still, I flailed and struggled, but Erini was too strong, too pumped up on her aspects. I didn't know how I could possibly defeat her.

No!

The voice came from within me, not my own. It sounded rich and womanly, a vibrant alto.

You must find a way. You must survive. You must fight. We cannot end like this.

We?

Who are you? I asked.

Whoever they were, they had a point. I couldn't die, not like this. I had too much to live for. I'd only just found true love — times three — each of my guys loving me in their own unique way. And I needed more time with my daughters. They might drive me crazy sometimes, but I still loved them and wanted to be the mother they deserved. And, speaking of being a mother, I had three new lives unborn within me. I had to live for them.

And I wanted to live for me too!

What can I do? I pleaded with the voice. I had almost no time left and I was barely conscious. My vision had contracted down to a couple of points of distant light filled with Erini's insane visages.

I don't know, the voice admitted, sounding a bit ashamed. *I've never fought Erini in her prime before. But we are a feared warrior. We can't be defeated by this upstart young godling. We should be far more powerful than she is.*

I've only just come into my aspects and she's been honing hers for centuries. I may have more aspects, but she's just too powerful!

Yes, you're right. A hesitant pause, then: *I've never done it before... but you can use your love to forge a bond with another willing soul,* the voice said softly, guiding me. *You need to bond with your men. You've already laid the groundwork, connecting to them with love. Seal the bond and you'll be able to share aspects with them, and they with you, all the time.*

Which meant, I'd be able to use my guys' aspects as

well as my own. That might just give me the edge against Erini.

I'll do it, I breathed internally.

I was no longer aware of the physical world at all, but I knew I wasn't dead yet, simply because I was still thinking. Even as the last of my awareness faded, I reached out with love and connected with my three daemon princes.

I felt Grey's stalwart and grounded soul. Ramsey's body may have been broken, but his spirit surged with hope and determination. Fen, though wounded and weary, possessed an endless well of kindness and generosity, a gentle strength, which belied his ravenous beast.

I spoke to all of them at once. *Will you join with me, bond souls with me, share everything you are with me?*

It was Ramsey who answered first. *Yes, my love. Everything I have is already yours.*

Grey spoke next, *If this is what you wish... Ana. I... my void... it is a terrible thing. Are you sure you wish to share it?*

Yes, if it means I get the rest of you as well. You are far more than your void, my love.

Then I'm yours, he replied.

Fen was hesitant. *My beast... it... how can you...? Ana, are you certain?*

I am. Give me your beast and I'll give you enough peace to quell it for eternity.

I felt Fen's astonishment. *Of course, my beloved. I should never have doubted you. Take everything I am and I accept all that you are.*

Then I proclaim it. We are one!

We are one, all three of them repeated after me. And with those words we bound our souls in love, everything we had, we shared with each other.

Suddenly I was filled with aspects ravenous and powerful: Grey's void and his ability to hunt and conquer, Ramsey's strife and conflict and raw physical power, and Fen's destruction and devouring, the insatiable hunger and the immensity of strength which reinforced it.

The tenacious fortitude I gained from my guys roused me back to awareness for just an instant.

But that instant was enough.

I surged healing into my arms, then reached up and pulled Erini's hands from my throat, as my vision returned. Instantly mending my throat, I filled my lungs with needed air.

"Time to send you back to Hades, bitch," I said with a grin, then punched her with all the pent-up power of war and strife and conquest and destruction. My fist connected solidly with one of her faces and caved in her cheek. That head bashed into the one next to it, and both seemed stunned.

I healed my legs and kneed her, but just for spite, I reached into her with my sex aspect and got her lady-lips all nice and super-sensitive before I drove my knee up between her legs.

The howl her three heads emitted was inhuman, but I didn't relent. I was going to make sure she couldn't hurt anyone else today.

I closed in and grabbed a fistful of hair from her two side heads and bashed them into the middle head.

That felt really good, so I did it again... and once more for good measure.

Erini stumbled, falling back, and landed splayed out. That made it easy to summon my sword and rid her of all her remaining limbs. I then healed her, just enough to stop the bleeding on those stumps so she wouldn't die. As I did, another of those bubbles of energy erupted out of her, trying to push me away. I swallowed it down with Fen's devouring.

She screamed and writhed in pain, but I wasn't done. I drove my sword through her stomach and into the ground. I healed around the wound so she wouldn't bleed internally, but she was trapped, pinned down.

I stood slowly.

"Had enough?" I asked. "Ready to submit?"

She screamed incomprehensibly, still flailing and trying to fight. Rays of destruction blasted out of her.

I erected a bubble of my own, using a mix of my peace and Grey's void, placing it around her. It stopped her beams instantly, keeping them contained. But she still blasted away for some time, unable to give up.

"She'll never willingly surrender, not when she's like this." Grey's voice behind me was calm and filled with his usual stoic power. "Use my void to siphon off her power, then she must be rendered unconscious. Only then will this end."

I glanced back. Grey leaned heavily on a tree, his chest wound still raw and open, but it was healing...?

Right. He had access to my healing now. Ramsey and Fen were getting up slowly as well and I felt their support, their love, their dedication, and their resilience filling me.

I nodded to Grey. "Thank you." Then I did as he'd said.

I opened my void to Erini and drank in the raging storm of her power. Adding a touch of Fen's devouring, I easily consumed Erini's hatred, jealousy, and destructive rage.

Still, she wouldn't give up. Her powers were gone, but she flailed physically, lost to madness.

I sighed and knelt, using my peace to fill her with serenity, binding it with law, even a little love. I didn't hate Erini. I pitied her. I couldn't fathom what it must be like to be constantly filled with rage, jealousy, and hatred.

Her body stilled, unconscious, eyes closed. She shimmered and the extra arms and legs and heads vanished. She looked like a normal, sleeping person. I removed my sword and restored her lost limbs.

With a heavy sigh, I stood.

But when the adrenaline of the fight faded, I was left utterly exhausted. My three men pressed in around me, holding me — holding each other — close.

"Well done!" boomed a voice from above us.

ANAIS

STARTLED, I LOOKED UP TO SEE A MAN WITH ASH-WHITE skin floating above us. Eyes like molten rock, red and seething, peered out from flowing locks of hair, some of which seemed red-gold in color, while other parts were black with crimson highlights. He was built solidly, with heavy arms and a broad chest.

Who the hell was this now?

"Shiva!" Grey called to the man. "What do you want?"

Shiva? That seemed to ring a bell, a Hindu god of... yeah, I had no clue. I really needed to learn more about the gods.

The man dropped from the sky, landing easily on strong legs.

"I'm not here for a fight," he said bowing to us. When he righted himself, his arms were out in a sign of surrender. "I'm here for her." He nodded to Erini.

"What do you intend to do with her?" I asked, curious.

"*And* if you were here the entire time, why didn't you stop Erini?" Grey said, harsh and accusing.

"Could he have?" I asked.

Fen answered. "Shiva is another Lord of Destruction, among other things, and as a true god with significantly more power than Erini, he would have been able to stop her, easily." He didn't sound happy.

I wasn't particularly happy to hear that, either.

"Yeah, why didn't you stop her?" I asked, matching Grey's tone from a moment ago.

"Because, this was your trial, Anais. Erini needed to do what she did, so you would become who you were meant to be, Goddess of Bonds." He bowed to me with a certain reverence.

"Wait... so this was all for me?"

Shiva nodded. "All true gods must pass a trial to come fully into their power. This was yours. It had to happen, somewhere, somehow, and of all the outcomes, this was the least harmful."

"*This* was the least harmful?" I glanced at the destroyed park around me, then back to the barely-standing hotel. "Wow. Fuck me."

Shiva smiled. "I have a wife with whom I'm quite happy. I believe you have others to perform that function, do you not?"

I blushed then. I blushed even more realizing I'd let my armor go and I was... yup... completely naked.

"Ah... yeah... well... thanks, I guess?" I said, summoning my armor to cover me again.

"You are most welcome, Anais, Goddess of Bonds." He peered deep into my eyes, his gaze penetrating deep into my soul. "And to you, Lady of Heaven." I had the feeling he wasn't talking to me.

No, he's talking to me, that other voice inside me replied.

Oh...

"Will you allow me to take her?" Shiva asked, indicating Erini. "It's my hope that with time and instruction, she can mend her ways and ease her troubled mind."

I looked to Grey since he was Erini's brother. "What do you think?"

He shrugged. "Hades hasn't worked for her, so it's worth a shot."

Turning back to Shiva, I said, "She's all yours."

He stepped in and lifted Erini carefully. "I bid you all a pleasant evening... though, for you it is far from over." Then he smiled and vanished in a swirl of blue smoke.

"Far from over?" I asked. "Anyone know what that means?"

"I believe I do," Raphael said as he landed nearby, folding his wings in behind him.

Oh fuck! I'd completely forgotten about Raphael... my father.

"Anais," he said softly as he came to me. "I think it's time you know the truth."

ANAIS

"Who are you?" Ramsey growled as he stepped protectively in front of me. "Other than one of Yahweh's little helpers."

"He's my father," I said softly.

All three of my guys turned to stare at me.

"Your father is a daemon prince? An archangel?" Grey breathed. "That explains a lot."

"And ah... I should probably mention now that Harmonia believes, my mother was... Inanna."

"That's correct," Raphael said with a smile and a dreamy, far-away look in his eyes.

Grey, Ramsey, and Fen all gaped at me. Grey recovered first.

"Of course..." he said as if everything suddenly made sense to him. "Your aspects match hers, except for healing and peace which—" he turned to Raphael, "—are yours, correct?"

Raphael nodded sagely.

"Why is that such a big deal?" I asked. I didn't quite understand why they were all so dumbstruck.

"Shall I explain?" Raphael answered.

"Yes, please do," I replied, then remembered I was wearing armor for clothes. "Though, can we do it elsewhere? I could use a change of clothes, as could most of these others." Then I realized I was being extremely selfish, remembering all the others who'd suffered this night. "Actually no, we should help the wounded and see if there are others in that mess of a building who need help."

Raphael held up a hand to stop me. "I wouldn't have come to find you if that hadn't been taken care of. Everyone has been brought out from the hotel, and those who could be healed, have been."

I caught on that wording. "Those who *could* be healed?" I asked.

"Some died. Mortals only, not that that minimizes it. I do have the power to return them to life, but not the authority to do so. Others, true gods, are handling that. Some were meant to die this night. Others will make a miraculous recovery."

"Oh... that's... horrid," I said softly. "Not people recovering, but that people were meant to die so that I could become who I am."

"Don't think of things that way," Raphael said as he approached. "I've been around for some time and have learned that not everyone can be saved. On this night, you were meant to become who you are... and some people were meant to die. It wasn't the one that caused the other, merely a mutual confluence of events."

That sounded less ugly, but I still felt awful.

"I need a bath," I whispered.

"If you wish to, you can transport us all to a place you feel is safe," Raphael said, his words slow, fatherly, instructive. "It is within your power to do so."

"Oh... really? How?"

He shrugged. "I've never been able to do it, but I believe it involves simply willing all of us to be elsewhere. Try it."

I drew in a breath, closed my eyes — I don't know why, but that felt appropriate — and envisioned all of us in Grey's living room.

There was a faint whisper of wind and then a more solid... something beneath my feet.

I opened my eyes to find myself exactly where I'd envisioned.

"Oh, wow," I breathed.

"Indeed," Raphael said. "You wished to change? Please do so. Then I'll tell you everything you wish to know."

I practically sprinted to Grey's room. I was filthy and really wanted a shower but didn't want to wait to hear what Raphael had to say. So, I threw on some yoga pants, a T-shirt, and one of Grey's fluffy bathrobes, then returned to the others.

As I did, I met my daughters in the hall.

"What's going on, Mom?" Reia asked.

Caia stood behind her, curious but quiet.

Eva was at the end of the hall peeking into the living area. "Who's the new guy? Another lover?"

I choked a little at that thought.

"Ah... no. That's Raphael. He's... your grandfather." I let that sink in and the three of them were silent for a moment until,

"He doesn't look old," Eva said. "In fact, he looks kind of cute."

"Eva!" I admonished her.

"What? He is. This whole *immortal gods* thing takes some getting used to, okay?"

She was right about that.

I sighed. "He was just about to tell me about himself and my mother," I said to my girls. "Did you three want to sit in?" They had a right to know as well.

They all agreed quickly, curiosity clear on their faces, so, the four of us went in and found places to sit.

Ramsey and Fen — whose clothes had been shredded — had wrapped themselves in blankets and sat at either end of one of the long couches while Grey remained standing, eyeing Raphael, who paced slowly until we were all ready.

"I'm all ears," I said.

Raphael stopped his pacing and smiled.

"Our story begins thousands of years ago, when early man began to place meaning and power in the elements around them and the emotions they felt, creating the first gods. One of these deities had many names in the early centuries, but when beliefs solidified, roughly ten thousand years ago, she was called Inanna."

Harmonia had said Inanna was one of the first goddesses, and the little research I'd done into Inanna had confirmed that she was ancient.

So far, none of this was news to me, but it was clear my daughters had questions, since this *was* new for them. Thankfully they kept quiet for now because I was sure there was a lot more of this tale left to tell.

"Sometime later... Yahweh came along and I was made manifest. But honestly, I'm not the important one in this story." How very humble of him... although Raphael *was* an *angel* and they were supposed to be humble.

"Time passed. Other gods came and went. Then about two hundred years ago, something miraculous happened. It was at the signing of the Treaty of Constantinople after the Greek War of Independence. Many gods and daemons were in attendance for that occasion, including Inanna and myself. I'd seen Inanna in passing over the centuries, but that was the first time we spoke at length." He let out a soft, contented sigh. "After that... we began to meet more often. Although always in secret."

"Secret? Why?" Caia asked.

Ramsey scoffed. "Angels aren't supposed to fraternize with other Empyreans. It looks bad."

Oh.

"Essentially, yes," Raphael said. "And Inanna in

particular wasn't seen in the most favorable light by my brethren."

"Ah." Yeah, a goddess of sex and war flirting with an angel. I could see how that might not go over well.

"Wait..." I said drawing out the word. "Wouldn't your Yahweh have known? Isn't he all-seeing and all-knowing or something?"

Again, Ramsey laughed, but it was Raphael who answered.

"As much as it's against dogma to say so, ah... no god is truly omniscient or omnipotent, though some do come close. Secrets can be kept from almost anyone if you're careful enough."

"Understood. Go on," I said, surprised that I was getting quite invested in the story. As much as most kids don't want to hear their parents' love story, I was fascinated.

"As I got to know Inanna, in addition to her beauty and love and... her many other charms, I began to notice a sadness about her. When I asked her about it, she told me that her love for me had revealed to her how much she'd become numb to the world. She was ancient, older than most beings, and she'd seen great loves come and go. But she'd also seen great wars and had lost her faith in humanity's ability to love."

I understood that. I didn't watch the news anymore because it all seemed bad these days. It seemed like people had forgotten how to love and care for each other.

"Then, about forty years ago, the two of us came up with a plan."

Oh! This is it, my story!

I leaned in, attentive.

"We would have a child, she and I." He looked at me with that glowing fatherly affection. "A girl." He took another long moment to admire me, then sighed softly. "But again, we had to keep everything secret. No one could know what we were doing. So, Inanna, as in tune with fertility as she was, decided to birth the child quickly, in secret. At the same time, Inanna would disappear. She spread rumors that she was feeling weak and faint, losing her strength. It isn't uncommon for some gods to just fade away into nothingness. We hoped people would think that's what happened."

I hesitated from asking why, hoping he'd explain.

"In truth, Inanna didn't die at all. She subsumed her existence into that of her child." Raphael looked at me. "She's within you, Anais." Then, like Shiva had done earlier, Raphael seemed to look through me, deep into my soul. "Hello, my beloved."

Warmth stirred deep within me.

So... *You're my mother?* I asked, seeking out that voice once again.

I am, Anais. I would say it's a pleasure to meet you, but I've always been with you. I've been a part of you every moment of your life.

Again, I wanted to ask why, but I held off. Instead, I simply said, *Hi, Mom.*

Hello, my dearest child.

The voice was cheerful and so full of love. It made me feel like I was wrapped in a warm blanket of motherly affection and tenderness. Tears welled in my eyes as I smiled.

"Our plan was for Inanna to experience the fullness of life, the brevity and immediacy of a human's existence," Raphael continued. "She wanted to know love and strife and heartache and motherhood so that she might reconnect with all of these things. But, in order for our plan to work, no one could know. Not even you, Anais. I'm sorry for that."

"Hence, my adoption records vanishing." I nodded.

"Indeed," he said, eyes filled with sympathy. "And it broke my heart that I wouldn't be there for you. But because of the secrecy around our relationship, I couldn't be the father I'd hoped I might be. That... pained me."

I could hear it, the agony in his voice that he'd had to stay away.

"I could check in on you from time to time, but no more." He came and knelt on the floor beside the couch where I sat. "Can you forgive me, Anais?" He clasped one of my hands in both of his.

I nodded. "Yes. Now that I know why, everything makes a lot more sense. Well, not everything, but my parentage and childhood make more sense at least. I forgive you, Raphael... Father."

And I forgive you, Mother, I said in my head.

Thank you, my dear.

"I'm glad," Raphael said with a smile. Then he tilted his head, looking curious. "That's most of my tale, but... there's more. Except I don't know the next part, Anais, only you do."

"Me?" I asked, confused. What did I know that he didn't?

"Yes. The plan was for you to live your life. Fully. Right through to your death of old age. Then after your death, Inanna would return and she would bring you back to life as our daughter. But... something went wrong. You were never supposed to tap into your aspects, never meant to have powers at all. We suspected some of our aspects might leak out and affect you in small ways. You never got sick, thanks to my healing, and your mother's fertility meant you couldn't stop getting pregnant. Not to mention your mother's sex going just a little nuts during your teen years."

"And twenties and thirties," I added with a sigh and nod.

"But beyond that, you were never supposed to have the powers you do now. I don't understand what happened," Raphael admitted. "It's a mystery to me how you came to be who you are today."

Silence hung over the group. If Raphael didn't know, I certainly didn't.

"Oh!" Grey breathed. Then he gave a louder and more significant, "Oh!" He blinked a few times at whatever realization he was having, then turned to us. "I think I know what happened."

ANAIS

GREY WAS SILENT FOR JUST LONG ENOUGH TO DRIVE ME crazy with curiosity. "What? What happened?" I demanded.

"When did you get that tattoo?" he asked. "The flower."

I blinked. "My tattoo?"

"Tattoo?" Raphael echoed.

"Tattoo?" my three girls said at the same time.

I wasn't going to show it to anyone because it was in a rather intimate spot. Still, for clarity's sake, I explained, "Yes, I have a tattoo. It's below my belly button."

Grey quickly picked up from there. "I always thought it felt... odd, from the moment I first saw it," Grey said. "A stylized rose, with eight petals." His gaze shifted to Raphael. "I'm assuming that means something to you?"

My father nodded slowly, still looking slightly confused.

"It does," he said softly. "It was our failsafe. If at any point humanity desperately needed Inanna to return, I could use that symbol as part of a ritual to bring her forth into the world again. It's a blending of a rosette and an eight-pointed star, both of which are Inanna's symbols." He looked at me. "And you got it as a tattoo? How? Why?"

I laughed a little at the strangeness of all of this. "That image has always been there, floating around in my head since I was a girl. I didn't know what it meant, but I'd seen it in my mind and in my dreams over and over. And when I decided to make a change in my life, I got it as a tattoo, a symbol of my new life."

That... may be my fault, Inanna said within me. *Just like our aspects managed to leak out of me into you, some knowledge of my symbols may have joined them.*

"Mom thinks it's her fault," I said without thinking.

It was only when everyone stared at me, that I recalled I hadn't told any of them about hearing a voice within me. "I ah... started hearing this voice... just recently... It's Inanna reaching out from within me," I explained.

Raphael smiled. "Yes, of course. She'd be awakening. How long have you had your tattoo?" he asked me.

"A couple months."

He nodded. "Sounds right. Since it wasn't done as the full ritual it wouldn't be instant, but the timeline seems logical otherwise."

"Timeline for what?" I asked.

Raphael laughed. "For Inanna to return to this world."

"Any idea when?" I asked Raphael as I posed the same question internally to Inanna.

Now, Inanna said within me. *I think I'm strong enough to return to the world. Be prepared my daughter, I don't know what this will feel like for you.*

Thanks for the warning, I said.

"Well," Raphael began. "I don't really know—"

"Mom's coming out," I interrupted him.

"Oh!" he said, eyes wide. Then he rose and stepped back as if I was about to explode. Everyone else joined him, moving back a little.

That didn't give me a lot of faith in what would happen next.

It felt... a little like being sick to my stomach. Something deep within me squirmed, then built and bubbled forth, rising inside of me. I gave a single, whole-body convulsion, then felt the essence within me leave.

And much of my godly power went with it.

An ethereal form billowed up from my chest and hung in the air over me. It looked like a ghost, vaguely feminine in form, and then it floated down, becoming more physical and real until one toe touched the ground, then a foot, and my mother was standing there before me.

She had dark lustrous hair, so very long and in perfect waves that covered her otherwise naked form... which was good because... Really, Mom?

It was clear I got my hair and eyes from Raphael, but my physique matched Inanna's: full and voluptuous.

She waved a hand down over her body and a gauzy dress appeared, covering her.

Thank the gods...

She looked around at everyone slowly, then finally turned to me. "I've seen you in the mirror so many times, but now... seeing you truly, for the first time, I'm overcome." Her voice was low and rich and choked with emotions as tears came to her eyes. "Anais, my daughter."

I rose and was in her arms a moment later, holding her tightly. "Mom," I whispered.

I'd finally found my mother and my father. All it had taken was a catastrophic event and nearly dying to find my birth parents.

An ancient goddess...

...And an angel.

Wow... yeah... I mean, I sort of thought I was special... but... wow.

"I feel emptier," I said, voice hushed, only for her. "Did you take your aspects back with you?" I pulled back a bit so I could see her face.

She smiled, spreading her full, dark lips, lending such softness to her features.

"No," she whispered. "All my powers and Raphael's are still within you. I simply needed a lot of celestial energy to manifest. It took a lot out of you. You'll recover in time."

Good, because I really wanted to keep my fertility aspect and expedite my pregnancy.

Also... I wanted to remain bonded to my guys.

And I was.

I could still feel the connection to each of them. Each of their souls was intricately bound to mine, making me sigh in relief.

Back when I'd not known who the voice within me was, she'd said, *I've never done it before... but you can use your love to forge a bond with another willing soul.* So, still in our muted tones, I asked, "Did you never bond with Dad?"

"No," she murmured. "I... as he said, I loved him and still do, but I was lost. I didn't wish to bind him to a lost soul."

"And now?" I asked. Had her time with me given her what she needed?

She kissed my cheek. "Now I have everything I need and my heart is full once again. Thank you for sharing your life with me, Anais."

A tear leaked from my eye and traced down my cheek. I hugged her close once again, and in that moment, she shared all her glorious love with me, and I felt truly at peace.

GREY

It was a lot to take in all at once. Ana had bound my soul to hers and as much as I had no qualms with that, it was still going to take some getting used to. I could *feel* her, feel what she felt, all the time. Add to that the revelation of Ana's parentage, and it was all a little too much for one night.

We all sought our various beds not long after Inanna emerged. Ramsey and Fen stayed with Ana and me, although we didn't do anything more than sleep in my large bed — yet another new one after last night's escapades. And because Raphael and Inanna still didn't want people to know of their relationship — at least for a little longer — they stayed at my penthouse in a guest room. My place was full now, no rooms left.

And there was no time to get used to things the next morning either. The conclave was still happening, and we all needed to be in attendance.

The Pierre Hotel had been remade by the next morning, and things moved on as if nothing had happened. The first order of business was finding out who had been responsible for the previous night's assault. Shiva came forward and spoke of Erini's tantrum and how he had her in custody at the moment.

And, of course, many of the more powerful or more celestially sensitive gods in attendance had felt the birth of a new goddess last night. There was a request for her to be brought before them and introduced, since new gods of such power were rare.

So Ana, looking radiant in a flowing gown of pale lilac — more conservative than usual for her — strode before the assembled gods and goddesses and introduced herself as The Goddess of Bonds.

She hedged and evaded any questions around her aspects, since that might give away who her parents were. We three men stayed close to her, all a bit over-protective, even though nothing of note happened. The gods accepted Ana and went back to their business.

Ana promised to keep in touch with Hera and Aphrodite, and even had a long — private — conversation with my mother, Persephone, who gave her blessing for our new union.

Soon enough, the conclave ended and life went on and we all finally got a chance to catch our breath and adjust to our new lives together.

Less than a week later, I sat in my office at the penthouse with various forms and papers arrayed in front of me.

It was late morning. Ana had slept in, but I felt her rousing, hungry, and I planned to get up and make her something for brunch in a moment, but I had other business to attend to first.

Caia, Ana's eldest daughter, arrived and knocked on the open door.

"You wanted to see me, Grey?" she asked.

I heard the hesitation. Ana had told all her daughters they could call Fen, Ramsey, and myself "Dad" if they wanted to, but it seemed Caia wasn't quite there yet.

"Yes, please have a seat." But as I said this I rose and motioned, not to the chairs on the other side of my desk, but the one I'd just been sitting in.

She cocked her head, curious as I moved around to the far side and sat in one of the other chairs. Caia shrugged and went to sit in mine.

"On the desk is paperwork. It outlines the handover of the Bio-Medical branch of Zagreus Holdings International from me to you."

Caia looked up, eyes wide, stunned. The two of us had talked business a few times, and I was thoroughly impressed with the young woman. Also, I desperately wanted to divest myself of all my businesses. I'd already handed full control of my financial branch over to Ana's Uncle Don. This was another step in offloading my responsibilities.

"Take a look over everything and sign where indicated. I have complete faith in you. Whenever we've talked, I've found you to be insightful, knowledgeable, and thoroughly inventive. It will take some getting used to, and I'll be there for anything you need, but I know you can handle this."

"Ah... wow... thanks?" she said, still in shock.

"I'm going to make your mother some brunch. Take your time and read everything over. If there are any terms you disagree with, let me know." I rose and smiled at her. "Sound good?"

She nodded and turned her focus to the many papers as I left.

I found Ana in the upstairs living area, hair still wet from a shower, tapping a pen to her lips, her little notebook out in front of her.

"You're hungry," I said. "I'll make some brunch."

"Grey, wait a sec," she called to me.

I nodded and sat next to her on the long couch.

Ramsey and Fen were both out at their jobs. Reia was at school, and Eva was taking some entrance exams for the New York Military Academy. Raphael and Inanna were still here, but they hadn't seen each other in years and mostly stayed cooped up in their room.

"What is it?" I asked.

She sighed. "I... I'd thought knowing my parents would tell me who I am. And it has, in a way..." She shook her head. "But for the most part... nothing's really changed... within me, I mean. I'm still who I was before all of this, just with a few more powers." She gave a soft laugh, shaking her head. "Fen was right. I was so certain that knowing my parents would help me know myself, but now that I'm thinking about it... why would it? I'm my own person. Knowing where you come from helps, but it can't tell you where you're going. Does that make sense?"

"It does." I nodded sagely. "It took me many long years to fully understand that I didn't have to be a man like my father. He was distant and uncaring and hard. I... I may come across that way to those who don't know me, but I like to think I've made myself a very different man."

Ana laughed. "Anyone who meets you at your office might think you're distant and hard, yes, but anyone meeting you at one of your shelters would see that you're a huge softy with a big heart and a bright smile."

I smiled. "Exactly. Knowing our parents only helps us figure out how much we want to be like them."

She nodded slowly. "From what I've learned about my parents, there are certain parts of them which are a little like me and others that I might want to emulate, but mostly, as much as we share aspects, I'm not like them in a lot of ways. They're both a little on the serious side and that's not me at all. I can be serious when I need to be, but I much prefer keeping things light. So... yeah... In a lot of ways, I'm back to square one, figuring myself out."

"What about your women's shelter idea?" I asked her. Several times since the conclave, she'd mentioned how she was pondering the idea of helping women get out of bad relationships and hopefully into good ones. "Isn't that something you want to pursue?"

She nodded. "It is, but I have a lot to learn about business first."

"Or you could let me handle the business end of things, at least at first, and you could just do the part you want to do."

"You'd do that?" Though even as she asked it, she laughed. "Of course you would. You're always telling me you'd do anything for me."

"Precisely. If you want to make this work, then *we'll* make it work... together."

She smiled. "Yeah. Together." Then her eyes opened wide. "Oh!"

"What?" I asked.

"Together!" she repeated. "What if Ramsey helped us with any *lawyery* things, and Fen could work in the kitchen or... or help the women retrain as chefs or construction workers or something. I... I think we could all make it work, don't you?"

I smiled and nodded. "Yeah, I think we could."

She leaned over to kiss me quickly. "Thanks! You're brilliant!"

"I'm pretty sure it was your idea."

"You inspired me."

"Sure." I kissed her back, a little longer, a little deeper, my hand caressing her thigh below the hem of her short skirt. I felt her arousal rise, billowing like smoke over embers within her and when I pulled back, I asked. "Did you want lunch or...?"

Heat flashed across her silver eyes and her desire

slammed into me like a steamy tidal wave, making me instantly hard and ready.

"I'll take 'or,'" she whispered, tossing the pen and notebook on the table and pulling me down onto her on the couch.

I didn't envy Fen and Ramsey, who'd be working away only to be hit by what I'd just felt... then hit with the even heavier wave of bliss I was about to induce in Ana. That thought gave me all manner of joy as I pleasured my true love beyond reason, knowing those two would feel every aching moment of it.

FEN

"I KNOW JUST THE PLACE TO BUILD IT!" I SAID WITH A GRIN.

I was as excited as Ana, about her new project. She'd mentioned it before, but now she was really going for it and I was happy to help.

"There's a project I was working on a little while ago. Some tech start-up bought four adjoining buildings in the east village to put in some trendy office space, but the bottom fell out of their business and we only got as far as demoing the inside. I bought the space from them for pennies on the dollar and it's been empty ever since. There's tons of space and you could make it whatever you wanted it to be since it's gutted at the moment. It'll take a lot of work to make it livable, but I'm on board, whatever you need Ana!"

Everyone was here, gathered around Grey's massive dining table, which had a few extra extensions in it at the moment. There were twelve of us: we three guys, Ana, her three daughters, Uncle Donny, and her parents, along with Eva's boyfriend Trent and his sister.

Ana had been telling us her idea about a place for women to go to liberate themselves from bad relationships, even if they had kids. Then Ana would help set them up for their new lives. It was perfectly Ana: a little war and law, a little peace and healing… and a whole lot of love.

"Oh, Fen, yes! That would be wonderful!" The joyous expression on Ana's face was everything to me. It would have been enough to warm my heart, but I already felt her intense gratitude and joy and excitement, which elevated my own emotions to a higher plane of existence.

"I'd love to help out once I'm done law school," Reia said with a wide grin. She turned to Ramsey. "If you'd be willing to have me on as an associate?"

Ramsey winked at her. "Hell yeah, kid! I know you'll be an amazing lawyer." He turned to Ana. "And yeah, I'm in. I'll help with anything you need, whether it's prosecuting dickhead husbands or softening them up a little to make sure they stay away from the women. Oh, and I know another lawyer who would love to help. She's a daemon named Aletheia, whose aspect is truth. With her in court, no man would be able to lie."

"Oh… wow, yes, if she's interested. I'd love to have her." Ana blinked. "I don't know how I'm going to pay for all of this. I mean, I know you're all willing to front some money to get things going, but it's not a business that's going to make much money."

"Those are called charities," Grey said. "You can get endowments and grants from all sorts of sources to help. Or... you could just ask the new head of Zagreus Bio-Medical to be your benefactor."

Everyone looked at Caia.

She was all business. "I'd be happy to help... after I've checked the books and analyzed our market readiness and profit margins. There are..." she trailed off seeing people's faces go a bit blank. "Ah... there are lots of details you don't care about that I'll need to look into, but yeah, I'm in."

"Zagreus Financial could also donate a substantial amount," Donny said with a grin. "Now that I've fired all those over-paid bank executives, we're finding we have a significant surplus."

"And if you need security, I'll have some army buddies once I'm done with my first tour," Eva said.

"If you need a mechanic, I'm in," Trent offered. He turned to his sister, Lisa, and smiled. She was the type of woman we'd be helping, having recently gotten out of a bad relationship with a guy who was connected up the wazoo.

Lisa piped up. "I have some administrative experience if you're looking for a receptionist or anything like that."

"You're hired, both of you," Ana said, her loving smile only getting wider and wider. "Trent, how would you feel about teaching women how to take care of their cars so they're not hustled by servicemen at dealerships or garages."

He nodded, excited. "I'd love to."

We were all excited. Even Raphael and Inanna — sitting hand in hand leaning on each other — were glowing with parental pride.

And for me... it would be a chance to finally create something instead of destroying things. And that thought gave me such hope and joy that I was close to tears.

Ever since I'd bonded with Ana, I'd been filled with so much peace that my wolf was practically dormant, happily resting.

My unending hunger was finally sated. It wasn't something I had to work to control anymore. And the weight that had been lifted from me was so immense I felt like I was walking on clouds, a bird soaring through the skies. Not only was I finally done with my beast, but I had the most incredible woman in existence loving me, and that lifted me higher still.

A few tears of purest joy might have slipped down my grinning cheeks in that moment.

After dinner, Raphael and Inanna retired to their room and the rest of us sat around and brainstormed for the new business, making plans and sharing ideas, even making a few calls to get things moving.

When Ana, Grey, Ramsey, and I retired for the night, she was literally glowing with joy, and vibrating with excited energy. And all of that was pumping into us three guys through our bond.

We took our time pleasuring Ana that night, full of

love and already over the moon with bliss. We held her and kissed her, then gave her a long soothing bath.

In bed, Ramsey and Grey lay on either side of her, kissing and caressing, while I pleasured her with my tongue, drawing out a long and relaxing orgasm from her. Then I cuddled in close behind Grey, feeling his warmth as I held him. He didn't pull away, didn't resist my affections, but I could still sense that that was all it was going to be. It might take some time before he was ready for more, but for now, he was comfortable being naked while near me and that was a pretty good start.

Life was perfect. I couldn't ask for anything more than this.

RAMSEY

HARMONIA, FREYJA, AND APHRODITE ALL JOINED ANA ON the day she'd decided to give birth. She'd waited a little over three months, letting the fetuses grow naturally while minimizing a lot of the discomfort that came with three growing bodies inside her. She hadn't wanted to have the children right away, said she wanted to feel them growing and savor some of the experience of pregnancy, and for those fifteen weeks, she'd been radiant and beautiful and already showing significantly by the end. Then, she'd decided, that was enough.

With three fertility goddesses there, the home birth was a breeze. Three crying babies later and Ana was resting on our bed, we three fathers each held our own tiny child... and it was clear right from the start whose was whose.

Merneith, my little girl, had my midnight-blue eyes

and had already torn through several sets of swaddling clothes. She'd be a fighter.

Fen's little boy, Wilf, shared his father's pale blue eyes and was constantly changing shape between a baby, a wolf cub, a lion cub, and a dove. That one was going to be a handful.

Then there was quiet, serious Elissa. She had Ana's silver eyes, but looking into them was mesmerizing as she possessed a hint of her father's void.

I stared down at Merneith, stunned from the moment she'd been put in my arms. I'd never thought I'd hold *my own* child. I'd always been a fighter, the Lord of Strife, and before Ana, my life hadn't had any room for a baby.

Then Ana had bonded with me and almost instantly stilled my chaos and conflict. I'd never known peace like this and, having lived with it for several months now, it was wonderful. I could summon my conflict for a court case if desired, but usually I didn't need it. I rarely went to the Empyrean Pits to fight. That held no interest for me anymore. Holding little Meri in my arms, I found a new and profound peace and love for this tiny being. She — and Ana — were all I needed.

The three goddess-midwives bid us goodbye and we three men with our little bundles climbed up onto the bed around Ana. She took them, one at a time, holding them, getting to know them, and feeding them.

"I can't believe I'm a mother... again... three times over. I'm not quite sure what I was thinking," she said, still in a bit of wonder-shock.

"You've given each of us the greatest gift," Fen said when he wasn't cooing to little Wilf. "We already know you're an amazing mother. And, like we said, we'll all be here to help with the little ones. My crew, both at the wrecking company and the restaurant can run fine without me most days. I'm so very happy to have another child."

"That's right, when we first met in that boutique store, you'd mentioned shopping for a daughter. But I've never seen you with her."

Fen laughed. "Ah... yeah, sorry about that. It was just the tiniest bit of a lie. I do have a daughter, but she's grown up and owns a modeling company in Sweden. She's not a child. She's... ah... seven hundred years old."

Ana gave a guffaw of a laugh. "Yeah, tiny lie, only a few hundred years off... but... you bought several dresses for a young woman that day."

"I did, yes. Then I gave them away to the daughters of some of my employees."

"All that just to meet me?" Ana asked coyly.

"It was worth it," he said with a wolfish grin.

"I never thought I'd have a child at all," I said, snuggling closer to Ana. "I didn't think one would fit in my life." I looked up and saw Grey nodding. He felt the same.

"And now?" Ana asked.

"Now... I may be the Lord of Strife, but it's a meaningless title. I've never felt so at peace. It's amazing. And when I look into Meri's eyes, all I can see is the father I want to be: kind and loving and giving."

"You aren't going soft on me, are you, big boy?" Ana teased.

"My heart has never been softer." I leaned down to kiss her forehead, then whisper in her ear. "Other parts of me are still rock hard and ready when you want them."

I felt her shiver of arousal, and it thrilled through all of us.

"Give a new mother a break," Ana said, her voice a little breathy. "I just popped out three tiny people and my lady-bits are a little sore and loose right now."

"Can't you heal?" I asked, wondering if perhaps this was something that couldn't be healed. I didn't think so, but I didn't know.

"Oh yeah, I'll be fine tomorrow," she said easily. "I just wanted to be sure we all knew there wasn't going to be any nookie tonight. Mama needs some rest."

We all laughed at that and each of us fathers put our child to sleep in their cribs. Ana sent them peace to soothe them and we all slept soundly after that.

The next morning, Grey was up early to make breakfast and Fen joined him. Those two had formed quite the bond over the last few months and were now a playful couple... which Ana loved. It wasn't my thing, though, and they'd respected that.

I'd been lying awake for some time, holding Ana close, her head resting on my chest, her warm body half covering mine as she slept in. When she stirred, she moved against me, squirming and shifting in ways that made my cock twitch and grow.

"Ooooh," Ana purred, voice still a bit groggy with sleep. "Big sexy man is holding me close." She kissed my chest, then ran a hand down over my abs. When her hand slipped below the covers, she brushed my aroused cock and laughed. "Have some sexy dreams, did we?"

She looked up at me, her eyes bright with mischief. Even with bedhead, she was gorgeous.

"Many," I said, then kissed the top of her head softly. "Also, you're really sexy when you're waking up, squirming and moaning and pressing your body against me."

"Oh, yeah?" she said with mock innocence while shifting against me even more. She slid up and onto me, those gloriously huge pregnancy tits pressing against me as she brought her face up to mine to nibble on my bottom lip. "Like this?"

I gave a low, heated chuckle. "If you'd like me to put another kid in you, keep going."

"That won't happen," she whispered. "I've turned off the baby-maker for now. I'm completely infertile until I *want* to have another kid, if ever."

"Oh?" I said, seizing her hips and rocking my own, bringing my cock up to brush against her core. "You don't say?"

She gave me a long, deep kiss, which made my cock ache with raging need to be buried inside her warmth. Then she shifted back a bit to rub her already wet pussy on my rock-hard shaft and sat up. I sent my hands up from her hips to those massive breasts, softly massaging, and she moaned and shivered as every aching spike of bliss caused by my kneading hands or her pressing clit tingled through me.

She was so close to an orgasm... when one of the babies began to cry.

We both laughed at our tense need for release playing against that persistent wail.

"Sounds like someone else needs these," Ana said, removing my hands from her breasts, albeit reluctantly, then slowly shifting off me and out of bed.

"Selfish little bastards," I said, joking.

Soon, the one child's crying had woken the other two and Ana had her hands full. I took Wilf into the bathroom for a diaper change while she fed Meri and Elissa. And so began our day... and many days to come.

ANAIS

GODS AND DAEMONS HAD COME OUT OF THE WOODWORK —
sometimes literally — to help me with my project. Ana's
House, as it was being called, had taken shape very
quickly. Between Fen's crew working hard and several
Empyreans with creation or building aspects, it was ready
by late spring.

A little over five months after I'd had the idea, we
opened.

The facility had over a hundred suites, some singles,
some for families, each with kitchens and luxurious bath-
rooms. There was also a cafeteria, a gym, daycare, laun-
dry, and even an indoor swimming pool. It was perfect.

I stood on the stoop at the main entrance, a crowd of
media and other curious folks gathered around below
me. Since this was a somber occasion, I wore a cream
blouse under a powder blue suit jacket with matching
long pencil skirt.

Grey, Ramsey, and Fen were here, but they'd stayed down in the crowd since this was my moment and they didn't want to overshadow it by looming behind me.

Harmonia had graciously offered to stay at home with the triplets. Having a nanny with the aspect of harmony was a godsend.

Caia, Eva, and Reia were also here, all beaming, so proud of me, and I knew Raphael and Inanna would be around, somewhere, watching.

They'd moved out of Grey's place and found a quiet cottage near Poughkeepsie, but we saw each other often enough, catching up for half a lifetime of lost time together. They still hadn't come out with their relationship yet, even though Raphael had said he didn't care if everyone knew, but still, they'd wanted just a bit more time together in secret, before it became a well-known thing.

I tapped the microphone before me and sent a screech of feedback through the speakers.

"Uh... sorry," I said, then cleared my throat and began. "Hello everyone, thank you for coming. We're here today to mark the grand opening of Ana's House."

I waved a hand toward the door behind me.

"Not long ago, I was in a horrible relationship, part of a pattern in my life. I managed to walk out with no worries, but that's not the case for many women in this city. They worry about their children. They worry about money and how they'll take care of themselves. They worry about a vindictive man coming after them. And it's for them that I created Ana's House. This state-of-the-art facility can house up to one hundred and forty-three women or families. All suites have the same amenities as a high-end hotel or condo complex, and everything here is provided for free, at no cost to the women who stay here. We can do that, thanks to many generous donations from philanthropic businesses. It's my hope that this can be a safe place and a place of healing for anyone who needs it." I looked directly ahead at the one camera set up before me. "So please, if you're in need of help, call the number you see on your screen. A small group will be sent, discreetly, to help you escape whatever situation you might be in. Thank you. Ana's House is now officially open!"

There were questions after that from the assembled reporters below, lots of questions, but I answered them all with ease. I'd been practicing.

Although, there was one that caught me off guard, "Is it true you are in a *polyamorous* relationship?" He made it sound like a scandalous thing.

I smiled at the man below me, who was clearly hoping to put me on the spot. I knew his type: righteously "moral" and superior, always looking down their noses and hoping to bring others down.

"I've been very lucky to find, not one, but three men who love me. I won't hide that fact. I'm truly blessed to have found such an abundance of love in my life." I turned toward that main camera. "And let it be known that Ana's House is open to any woman or those who identify as women who are seeking solace, no matter what type of relationship you were in or hope to be in. We're a caring and accepting home for any who need a little help. Next question."

I slapped that reporter with a wallop of peace to shut him up and moved on.

Finally, there was an official ribbon cutting with lots of pictures and that completed the formal opening ceremony. After that, I led the press through a tour, which ended with a small reception lunch, and then everyone left.

Later, that afternoon, I sat up in my office, looking at our funding projections, wondering how long it might take before word spread.

My phone buzzed with a text. I looked and saw Trent's sister Lisa — our receptionist — asking me to come down to the main reception area.

I arrived to find three families already here, and the phones ringing off the hook. Lisa looked a little frazzled so I helped with the intake of the families while she answered the phones.

By the end of our first day, we had five women or families already living with us and we'd be sending our "extraction teams" to pick up a half dozen more overnight.

I was stunned and thrilled that we were helping so many so soon, even though I was saddened that so many needed such help.

That evening, I left things in the capable hands of my

dual night managers: Krystal and Maera, two of the daemons I'd worked with at Elysium. They'd wanted to help and were used to working late.

I was no longer living at Grey's Penthouse. The renovations were done on the brownstone, and... it was truly mine now. Uncle Don had seen how much I'd changed and transferred ownership to me. He'd moved out and was now living closer to the financial district where he worked.

It had been a long and exhausting day, so I let Ramsey carry me up the stairs to our room. We relieved Harmonia of babysitting duty, though she didn't look that tired, even after a long day taking care of three demanding infants.

"You'll need to find another daemon to look after them," she said. "As much as I'd love to be a full-time nanny, I'm still running Elysium."

"Anyone you'd suggest?" I asked. Harmonia's aspect made her ideal for looking after three super-powered toddlers.

"I could see if Eirene is interested," she said after a moment's thought. "I hear she's getting tired of trying to make peace in the Middle East. She might be up for something different."

I still didn't know enough about all the gods and daemons. "And she is?"

"A daemon of peace, and a kind-hearted, long-suffering, good-natured woman."

I smiled. "If you could reach out and see, that would be great."

"I'll let you know," Harmonia said, then kissed me on the cheek. "Take care."

I saw her out, then returned to the others. It was already late evening by then, and we'd all eaten before getting home, so we began our nightly routine. Bottles of breastmilk were warmed and we fed the triplets as we got ready for bed. I was half out of my clothes when I stopped to admire my three amazing men.

Fen was whispering a story to Elissa and Wilf while they cooed and dozed in their cribs, Grey was stripping out of his suit, and Ramsey, who was naked from the waist up, was cradling Meri while feeding her. The big man was so kind and gentle and peaceful. Seeing him fawn over his daughter made my heart swell. Also... there was nothing sexier than a half-naked, thick-muscled, manly-man being so tender and loving to a child.

Even as my heart was filled with delight at the sight, my core was heating with bubbling intensity. My guys had been perfect today — like they were every day — and they were going to get lucky tonight.

"You know we can feel that, right?" Grey said, coming to me.

He was ready for bed... which meant stark naked, and his cock was half-aroused, twitching and growing. He stroked my hair and cupped my cheek, kissing me softly before helping me undress.

"Feel what?" I asked, with mock innocence.

"Our sex goddess getting horny," he breathed, kissing my cheek.

His hands slid over my hips and pushed off my skirt, leaving it pooled at my ankles and me naked. He pressed himself behind me, strong arms around me, slowly caressing my suddenly sensitive skin and I leaned into him with a contented sigh.

"Make sure the kids are asleep," Grey murmured as he kissed my cheek.

I nodded, floating on a cloud of serene pleasure. I took the peace and joy I was feeling and let it wash over the three tiny beings. Elissa and Wilf stopped their stirring and cooing and settled. Meri drained the last of her bottle and was instantly asleep in Ramsey's arms.

"Done," I whispered even though I didn't really need to whisper. Once the triplets had been put to sleep in such a way, nothing would wake them for at least a couple of hours. We four could be as loud as we wanted and not risk waking the kids.

"Good," Grey breathed against my ear, and one of his caressing hands came up to press and play on my more-than-ample bosom. I moaned and began a slow squirming against him, feeling his cock harden against my back.

Ramsey put Meri in her crib, then turned to watch us as he got out of his pants.

He stroked his massive cock for a moment as he asked, "Do you want alone time or all of us?"

I smiled. My guys had all become so very accommodating. They didn't mind if I wanted to spend some time with just one of them or a pair, or all three together, whatever I wanted or needed, that's what they gave me.

I held a hand up to Ramsey, indicating I'd get back to that question. Turning my face to the side, Grey leaned down and captured my lips in a long, slow, sensual kiss that made fireworks go off in my heart and sent fizzy bubbles of tingling bliss through every other part of me right down to my toes.

"If you and Fen want to give me a show," I said against Grey's lips, "I promise to reward you after."

Grey gave a wide smile and nodded. "Anything for you," he whispered and kissed me lightly before sweeping me up in his arms and carrying me over to Ramsey. "She's all yours for a bit, but make sure she can see us."

Ramsey chuckled. "Oh, we're doing *that*, are we? Sounds good." He carried me over to the bed. "How do you want me?" he asked, laying me on the thick bedding.

"Sit with me, hold me, touch me," I said.

He joined me on the bed, a bit behind and beside, and began by kissing my shoulder as his large hands moved over me.

Meanwhile, Grey was helping Fen out of what remained of his suit, slowly, sensually. The two of them shared kisses and soft caresses, their muscled bodies close and brushing.

Gods, but they were sexy. I couldn't believe how far they'd come, or that they were even willing to be with each other at all. I knew Fen had instigated it and Grey had been grudging at first, but now... the two of them were lovers in their own right, and watching them was so very... steamy. I hadn't even thought I'd like this sort of thing... but I did... a lot.

Their lips brushed and tongues tasted as their hard bodies pressed against each other. Grey's hand combed through Fen's long golden locks as their mouths merged in a needful kiss, and I was quickly going from pleasantly buzzed with bliss to a steamy, wet mess of quivering need.

Ramsey placed soft kisses down my arm, then over the fullness of one breast as his hand caressed my thigh with long brushes from tentative fingers. Each stroke slid closer to my core, but he was taking his time, making me want his touch on my folds all the more.

Fen slid out of his boxers, freeing his long cock. I loved to watch those two rigid shafts brushing by one another as Grey and Fen pressed themselves together. Fen's hand slid down Grey's muscled flank to the high, round tautness of his ass, gripping firmly as their loins pressed together.

And that's when Ramsey brushed a single seeking finger over the liquid-fire of my folds. I opened to his touch instantly, and with a shivering gasp-moan, I came in a soft, trembling orgasm.

But still, Ramsey didn't dive into me right away. He'd cooled a lot from the raging passion he'd possessed when we'd met. He could still be that rough and needful beast, but he could also be slow and playful, as he was now.

His one finger traced slowly around my soaked folds, and I savored every searing touch as his mouth found a nipple and sucked softly. It wouldn't take much for me to give him a squirt of breastmilk since I was still lactating and he was very good at teasing my nipple to receive such a treat.

I was trembling, my entire body on fire with an urgency of passion, a new and heavy wave of pleasure sweeping me up toward a much more powerful orgasm. I just needed a bit more.

Fen kissed his way down Grey's hard body then grabbed the other man's cock as he knelt, his long tongue lapping out to lick Grey's twitching shaft before Fen took him fully into his mouth.

At the same time, I put my hand over Ramsey's, pressing his finger to my clit while I rocked my hips a bit, tweaking myself. He got the hint and was soon rubbing me hard. I fell back into Ramsey's other strong arm, shaking with a shout of bliss as my orgasm pounced on me, raking claws of pure pleasure down my body in shivering waves.

"Okay boys," I called out, voice quavering. "Enough foreplay!"

Ramsey laid me back on the bed, his lips coming to mine, the taste of my milk still on them. Then he flipped a switch and went from soft and teasing to hard and seeking, and his tongue drove into my mouth, claiming it.

"I need you," he breathed his voice ragged when he finally tore his lips from mine.

This was the challenge with my bond to my guys. When I was horny, so were they, and when I got off... they got ramped up to the extreme really quickly, even if they'd wanted to take their time. Usually, I used my sex aspect to cool them, keeping them primed and ready as they pleasured me, but tonight, I wanted to feel all of Ramsey's hard, possessive thrusting.

I opened my legs as he slid over me. "Take me," I whispered to him.

Grey and Fen were climbing onto the bed on either side of us, and I used my sex aspect on them, sealing off their bliss, capping it, and making sure they wouldn't come when they felt what Ramsey was about to do to me.

Ramsey drove his monster cock into my more-than-ready pussy and I gushed around him, helping him glide deeply into me.

I knew he wouldn't last long, and I didn't want him to. I pushed sex into both of us, driving us mad with lust.

Ramsey reared back, eyes wide, pupils enlarged as he took me in, mouth gasping for air. His strong fingers dug into the top of my hips, and I locked my legs around him, keeping me in place while he drove himself relentlessly into me.

Fen and Grey, lying on either side of me, kissed my face and shoulders and breasts, and I wrapped my arms around them keeping them close, my bliss skyrocketing with each of Ramsey's possessive thrusts.

Ramsey slid a hand down, thumb dropping over my clit, and rubbed it as he swelled, nearing his climax.

My first two orgasms had been teasers, a hint of what I felt now as that thumb on my clit sent rockets of orgasmic ecstasy blasting through me.

I came, crying out, writhing and pushing Fen and Grey's faces into my tits. My pussy clenched and milked the giant cock inside me and Ramsey couldn't take any more. He drove deep and unleashed his hot torrent, filling me. My body drank in his release, my orgasm pulsing and pushing it deeper within me, and it was a good thing my fertility was turned off because he was filling me to the brim.

"Fucking gods," Ramsey breathed, then he laughed, realizing what he'd said. The convulsions of his laughter sent new spikes of pleasure through me, and I tried to laugh with him, but it came out more as panting, moaning gasps.

Grey and Fen were also moaning heavily. They'd felt all of my explosive, powerful orgasm but hadn't been able to get off. Their cocks had to be aching painfully, throbbing with their own need.

Thankfully, Ramsey's passion was so stoked he drained himself, finishing quickly. Then he withdrew and knelt before me, kissing my flower tattoo.

It was something they all did now: kissing the flower and whispering, "Blessed be my beloved." A form of worship at the altar that was my body.

With a satisfied groan, Ramsey flopped back along the bottom of the large bed, repeating "Holy fuck," then laughing after each iteration.

Despite the massive tidal wave of pleasure surging through both Fen and Grey, they didn't try to take Ramsey's place right away.

Instead, Grey remained where he was, shifting up to kiss my lips while his hands massaged my oh-so-sensitive breasts. Fen kissed his way down, and I knew I was about to get one of his signature tongue lashings. And when his miracle tongue slid over my wet folds and flicked over my clit, I had a mini-orgasm, gasping into Grey's mouth.

Fen was slow, savoring my pussy, keeping me at the heights of ecstasy until I couldn't take it anymore.

Desperate, I pushed Grey back.

"Now!" I begged, hoping they understood.

And they did. They knew exactly what I needed.

I was lifted and shifted until Grey was behind me, kneeling with his legs together and Fen was in front, kneeling with legs apart. That meant they could get really close as I was lowered onto two waiting towers of rigid flesh, filling me front and back.

Fen kissed my lips softly, while Grey kissed my hair, then they shifted and kissed each other over my shoulder, which was so amazingly hot.

Ramsey came to my other side, claiming my lips, and I ground down onto Fen's shaft as he and Grey plunged into me with a hard and insistent rhythm, making every cell in my body sizzle.

I knew they were aching, knew they felt everything I felt and still hadn't come yet, and I also knew they wanted to drive me completely insane with bliss before I released them.

They separated from each other and began covering me with wet kisses. Grey, reached around to lift my heavy breasts so Fen could kiss and pluck at them, and I was so aroused that even just a faint teasing of my nipples caused miraculous mini-orgasms to roll through me.

When Fen looked up at me, his face was pained with such extreme pleasure, tears dampened his cheeks.

"My goddess!" he cried out. "Too sexy, too gorgeous, too ravishing... too fucking much!"

His cock swelled and twitched through a powerful orgasm. Except he didn't come, not yet, because I still held his release.

The aching pressure of his wolf's knot stretched me, driving me even crazier with bliss, and his hands around the back of my neck kept him locked in place, his gaze always on mine, letting me know just how much I'd completely overwhelmed him.

I saw the aching, powerful, painful urgency written on his features and in his aqua-blue eyes, and I reached out my arms, drawing him close, squirming my breasts against his hard chest as I brought my lips to his ear.

"You're welcome," I whispered, and I finally released him.

Fen's body instantly stiffened and his cry of rapture sailed up through several octaves before becoming completely inaudible. His cock blasted his release and the power of it filled me, not only physically, but spiritually and I was blown open with a release of my own.

Behind me, I heard the panting, pleading, needful voice of Grey.

"Please, goddess!" he begged, and I released him too.

He exploded within me with a long, loud moan.

That sound and the feel of his hot surge sent another heavenly orgasm bursting through me. More than that, the rapture Fen and Grey felt also filled me through our connection. I reverberated my pleasure back out to them in an ever-escalating wave of euphoria that blew all of our minds.

Ramsey rose, bringing his fully aroused cock to my lips, his eyes pleading, seeking permission. I already had my mouth gaping in a silent scream of pure joy, and I nodded to him. He slid his revitalized cock between my lips and, despite having had a powerful release only a moment ago, pulsed forth again, filling my mouth. He'd felt everything the rest of us had just felt and couldn't help but come again.

We stayed that way, clinging to each other, throbbing and shivering through the very slow descent back to normal.

Ramsey finished and collapsed on the bed, but it took longer for the rest of us to move. We were practically merged into one, bodies stiff and sore and plastered together with sweat.

Fen in particular was locked inside me with his knot until he was fully and gloriously spent. Then he slowly withdrew, shuffling back, while Grey leaned back, taking me with him so Fen could give his blessing, kissing my tattoo.

Once Fen was resting, Grey and I slowly drew apart. He shifted around and kissed my flower as well, whispering, "Blessed be my beloved."

Then we all lay in an exhausted heap, panting and regaining ourselves for a while.

It occurred to me then... this was going to be my life... forever. Having fully come into my goddesshood, I was immortal now. I wouldn't age, and neither would my men. My children would grow and leave home and I'd still be here, with three amazing men who showed me just how much they loved and adored me every day and every night... forever.

"I'm the luckiest woman in the world," I whispered. "I love you all so much and... and I *know* you love me. I feel it, every hour of every day. I can see how much you love our children and..." I was rambling, but I didn't care. "I can't believe this is going to be my life... forever."

"Believe it, Silverlocks," Ramsey whispered. "And you're not the only lucky one."

"Yeah, but there's only one of me and three of you. I get three times the love and—"

"And...!" Fen cut me off. "We're lucky because we get to be with a fucking love goddess. Ana, you may think you get three times the love, but what each of us gives you is amplified and sent back to us ten times over."

"Ten times?" Grey scoffed. "For me, it's more like fifty times."

"It's a hundred times for me," Ramsey said, playing along with their one-upmanship.

I laughed. "Really?"

Fen had this way of being so very earnest and serious at just the right time. Now was one of them, and there was no exaggeration or joke in his voice when he whispered, "Really, Ana. You're that powerful. So... let's all agree... we're all fucking lucky."

"Agreed," I said with another laugh. "You guys are amazing!"

"We're all amazing,' Grey said, snuggling up close behind Fen, who was snuggling up to me.

Ramsey pressed close on my other side. "Fucking right we are."

I fell asleep that night overflowing with love. A perfect end to a wonderful day, and the perfect start to my new life... as a goddess.

OTHER BOOKS BY TESSA COLE

NEPHILIM'S DESTINY

ANGEL'S FATE

ENSNARED BY THE PACK

Claiming Demons, book 3